B[

UNI\

Death of a Nightingale

Annika Pampel

ISBN 9791220153041
First edition: September 2024

Death of a Nightingale

"For all of you who find light in darkness."

TABLE OF CONTENTS

A PROLOGUE ABOUT A GHOST

 Let's talk about the forgotten romance of poetry. Shall we?

> Last night upon the stair,
> I saw a man who wasn't there.
> He wasn't there again today.
> Oh, how I wish he'd go away.

Now, this particular gem has always been a favorite of mine. In four little lines, it frightens us of an intruder, already within our house. When my father used to tell it to me, an avid poetry fiend, by the way, I always thought it referenced a ghost. A revenant of a lost soul, who had passed with unfinished business.

Many, many years later, I think it speaks of something entirely different. You see, dear reader, the author of this little joyous beast named it "The Antigonish Poem," which roughly references the anguish of losing someone most dearly beloved. A mother, a father, a child, or a lover.

I believe, having been alive longer than anyone I know, it speaks of oneself. Every time you lose someone dear to your heart, it breaks in two. And even though it heals, you lose a little piece of yourself to the ones you gave it to. A sliver of your precious self will always be with those you lost. And if you should meet them again, or their memory flares by, you recognize yourself. The forgotten pieces.

So, alas, the man, or in my case, it would be a woman, sees a reflection, a remanence of herself as she used to be, once, long ago. A ghost of a different kind. A shadow of a forgotten part of self, scaring her into submission.

Shall we submit, then, to the haunting echoes of our past? Shall we confront the apparitions of our own making, the ethereal remnants of who we once were? In the dim corridors of memory, where the flickering candlelight reveals the specters of bygone selves, we may find solace or be ensnared by the phantoms that linger within. For in embracing the ghosts we've become, we may unlock the secrets of our own haunted hearts. Shall we, dear reader, embark on a journey of darkness?

CHAPTER 1: WELCOME TO THE NIGHT

I can hear the water dripping. Drip. Drip. Pause. Drip. I don't like it. The water, an ethereal conductor in this spectral orchestra, plays a disconcerting melody, one that unnerves my every sense and mocks the very concept of solace. At least be reliable in your rhythm. Drip. Pause. Pause. Pause. Drip. I focus on it. And all of a sudden, it's shy. Utter silence. My eyes narrow. I wait. Has it stopped raining through the remaining parts of the glass? A minute passes. Any statue would envy my stillness. No move, no breath. I scan the ceiling. It's quite beautiful.

An old greenhouse, I suppose. A large chapel dome spans across, barely containing the rudeness of the weeds and rubble that have taken over this long-forgotten glory. Most of the rusted frame remains. Like a skeleton, holding a few last pieces of glass between them. The haunting beauty of decay weaves a narrative of its own, mirroring my calculated choice of an unconventional stage for my somber performance.

Drip. There you are. I smirk. As if the water was taunting me. Playing a very dull game of 'hide and seek'. I shake my head at myself and the movement makes me sway. I've been hanging here for a while. The rope makes a musical sound, not quite a squeak. Back and forth. I encourage it to swing wider. I was particularly clever with this attempt and hung myself in the middle of the room.

For most people, it would have done the trick. With one step down, the rope would have tightened into a snap, breaking the neck and just gently lilting a body into oblivion. What a thought. Oblivion.

For me, it did no such thing. The step down was calculated. The deepest part of this stunning, dilapidated structure. I stepped, the rope snapped and creaked, and then I swung until I stopped in stillness, looking at peeling wallpaper, listening to the drip.

Drip. I laugh. It is indeed taunting me. And now, I can't reach the wall to free myself and try again. Note to self: If you're not sure that it will actually kill you, give yourself a less awkward escape route. I sway some more and stretch out my arms to hold on to the vines of greenery. Almost. So close. And...said greenery is also not on my side and breaks off in my hand. Now I'm holding, what looks like an odd wedding bouquet while hanging in frustration.

I realize, to my horror, that I've been quite rude. I entirely skipped introductions. My name is Graciella Lucard. Let's make that a bit shorter and more time appropriate. Just call me Grace. I would like to clarify that I don't joke about suicide or take it lightly, by any means. I have some very specific reasons for my choice. And once I'll tell you, you might even agree with me that a world without me is much better off.

I stretch out boldly and grab the rope upwards with my feet. Yes, I'm athletic, you could say. More than that, actually. It wasn't always like that though. My favorite past-time was studying with my father. Dr. Tepēz Lucard. He was a truly wonderful man. Even for that time. He encouraged me to learn and research his favorite field of medicine and let me assist in autopsies.

Finally! I manage to remove the noose over my head and shake out my long hair. Upside down. For a moment I feel free. I angle my head and look at the floor. Old, intricate furniture, broken by weather and abandonment. Just like any heart would be.

Forgive me, we were talking about dead bodies. My father firmly believed in science. He wanted me to learn as much as I could to be the master of my own destiny, even as a woman. Times were a little different back then. He was also an immigrant. I never heard the story. He was very quiet about the circumstances that made him run away from Europe. But he did. Left our entire family behind to be with my mother and raise my sister and me.

Every other night, we stole a body from the local village cemetery and examined it for possible causes of death. Back then ninety percent of people died of consumption. It was a pretty safe guess. The giveaway: pale, paper-thin skin, red lips, sometimes with a bit of blood still oozing from them, hollow cheeks, and bright, frightened eyes.

The villagers didn't agree with that diagnosis, of course. But we'll have to forgive their ignorance. You see, my new friend, people back then didn't know how bodies decompose. It wasn't yet studied. So when they looked at a corpse and the gasses inside caused it to quite suddenly pop up to sit and stare at them, nails still growing, hair still growing, bloody lips, what do you believe their first guess was? Not consumption, I can assure you. I've seen it many times, that they were so scared, that they staked the corpse to its casket, ensuring it never rose from the grave.

In hindsight, that seems incredibly silly. Turns out, stakes really ain't gonna do it. They're a nuisance, don't get me wrong. You're gonna be busy twisting it out in very tight confinement, cursing colorfully without anyone to enjoy your naughty vocabulary, and after all that, which can take days, by the way, you have to dig yourself out of six feet of dirt. Not fun. But more like hanging yourself in the middle of a very tall room, definitely not deadly.

And that, my new friend, is the problem. Nothing seems to be deadly. As you may have gathered, I am immortal. I can tell you that eternal life is highly very overrated. But let me show you why so you can draw your own conclusions. Come along, we're already late.

CHAPTER 2: ANGEL OF DEATH

Let's visit some friends of mine. Shall we? I want to show you that once you know me, you would want me to die too. But I'll leave any judgment up to your discretion.

The city is lovely around this time. Just before midnight. It's rainy and doused in fog. The newer buildings reach through the mist like a giant's hand. The old German expressionists would adore this look. A dreary metropolis in the new world with remnants of Anglo-Saxon influence; Atlanta. Southern in some ways. Look and culture. But also something more. It's not the Charleston, wrap-around-porch kind of southern. This is the place where crazy traffic meets urban decay and underground gargoyles.

Tonight the rain pummels the pavement. Licking it clean of the daily, human hustle. I always wonder why everyone is in such a hurry. Where are they all going? Do they ever arrive? As I get off the station in Alpharetta I only see a lonely rat scurrying for cover. Cautious, little critter. But, to be fair, rightfully so. I'm starving and I don't discriminate.
The hospice care facility already looks like a funeral home. Is that supposed to help its inhabitants prepare for their future? I never understood. The red brick is broken up by white columns and a little A-frame awning. I bee-line for the backdoor. Thankfully it's never locked. Easy access.

The hallways have that lovely, cheerful asylum smell and washable paint on the walls. In case things get messy. You have to give it to the medical professionals, they always know how to keep things upbeat and positive.
Today I already know where I'm headed. Room 407, last door on the left. I chuckle. She left it ajar for me in anticipation. How presumptuous. I usually like to be a surprise. But, I enter regardless.

"Didn't you tell me you were going to be dead by this time today?" A croaking voice rattled with cancer all the way up her throat. Susanna glares at me. For a lady on her death bed, she sure still has some fight in her.

"I gave it my best shot," I reply, as she already pulls out a deck of cards and sits up. "You've got to be more committed. Look at me, this is how you die." She coughs. It's pitiful, but I give her a smile and sit down. "One last game?" She asks and my eyebrows rise sky-high. "Last game? You want me to kill you tonight?" I ask politely, but I already know the answer. She's been begging me to take her life for over a month. Always over a game of Black Jack. "Better you, than the cancer." She replies and deals me in. Two cards are next to my hip on the blanket. "I tell you what, old lady, you win, you get to die tonight. Deal?" She looks me up and down.
"You might look like a 19-year-old girl, but we both know who the crone really is." She whispers. I can't help myself and smile as I cover my mouth, signaling her not to speak of it. As though I'd be insecure about my age. I don't care. The years don't touch my shell. Only my heart. But we already established that, haven't we.
I flip the cards over and put on a carefully blank face as I stare at a lousy four and a two. I give her a dead-eyed look. "Did you plan to give me shit cards?" Susanna tries to laugh, but her chest heaves like a broken engine. I can feel her pain reverberate through the room. Even from my standpoint, cancer sucks. I squeeze her hand. It's cold already.

"Another?" She manages to get out. I nod and she gives me a ten and skips the round herself. Not having looked at her own cards. Well, what a predicament. I'm at sixteen. A shitty position. I probably need another card, but it'll be oh so easy to go over the allotted twenty-one. On the other hand, she hasn't even checked what she has. She grins. Somehow it's maddening. She was probably a ton of fun when she was younger. I would have liked her.

She tilts her head and asks me: "Should I turn my cards and then you decide whether you want another one?". I give the woman a blink. "Sure, I'll take whatever you offer." I say back as she flips over two tens. Damn.

Now I have no choice. My hand beckons for another card as I shake my head. She looks at me with sincerity as I turn over my hand. My four, two, ten, and ...an Ace of hearts. She smiles at me with relief. "And I'll take what you offer, child. Death on swift wings."

I nod. Fair enough. She won. She asked for it. Who am I to deny her. I ease her into her pillow, which I fluff up with my other hand. I stroke over her bandana-covered bald head with a tender hand as I take out my favorite, curved scalpel. It was my father's favorite tool to use during autopsies. With a single stroke, you could open up a corpse from hip to sternum. "Tell the angels I said hello." I tell her as I let the sharp tip of the blade enter her neck. I'm precise. Had a lot of practice.

As I taste the first sweetness of her sickly blood, giving release to us both, she croaks: "You know they don't want to hear from you. Angel of death." I smile, teeth covered in her blood. She rasps a laugh, looking at my silver eyes. They change when the real me comes out to play. She's in awe I think. "They're a bunch of judgmental elitists. Say hi anyway." I finish talking, too distracted by my own hungry needs, and lower my mouth and teeth back to the small wound I created at her carotid artery. I drink, ignoring the foul taste the cancer has given her. It won't kill me. And if it does, we both won. I lose myself. The warmth, the gulps. There's a flow to it. The flow of life that enters me when I feed. It always does and I love the ecstasy it fills me with. I love it so much, I could keep killing and killing and killing some more just for sport. It drives me wild.

19

But her frail body slumps lower into her pillow as her jaw slacks open and her eyes lose their shine. She's gone. I look at her for a moment and tenderly close her mouth and eyes. Goodbye Susanna. May you enjoy oblivion before I do. Like all the others.

I leave the cards. Her last game can be found with her. They'll know she had a bit of fun. As I turn right towards the exit, I hear a pair of heels behind me and I freeze. "Leaving so soon?" It's a cheery voice to be sure but it has an edge to it. My heart skips a beat. Do I have to kill her too? The clicks of her heels approach closer. Her voice right behind me. "I take it Susanna is at peace?"

That gives me pause. She knows. I turn, hoping my teeth aren't bloody anymore. Yes, even I have basic manners. One doesn't speak with their mouths full of food. She's small in stature. Robust. Middle-aged. She wears those silly half-high four-inch heels that make anyone look old and sexless. Her once blond bob needs a touch-up. The grey roots give away her decline.

She extends a hand. "Dorothy, Chief Nursing Officer. Nice to finally meet you, Grace." I'm flustered. If she knows who, what I am, is this woman out of her mind? She's giving me her hand? But something within me, be it politeness or amusement returns the gesture. We shake hands. "You know of me." I state the obvious.

Without an inkling of fear she smiles. "I make it my business to know what's happening with patients under my care." Oh no, I think I do have to kill her. My eyes dark to her soft neck. A bit thick to find the veins swiftly. This one might hurt her. I don't like it when they scream in pain. It's always so screechy. "I think you should return Friday." She finishes with a nod to the door on the left. I blink. Unable to hide my surprise. Immortal or not, apparently this woman rendered me speechless.

Congratulations to her. That is a tough thing to accomplish.

"Assisted suicide is still illegal in this country. Even for patients, who suffer a great deal of pain. You seem to...have a special talent, that can help us with that problem." I think my mouth is open in utter surprise. Kitten-heels nurse lady wants me to come back and kill people? Wow. This night is getting stranger by the moment. Dear reader, I'm glad you came along to witness this, otherwise, it would be hard to believe. I try to start forming words, but I still have none. She looks me up and down. "If you can, of course. I don't know how often you...eat." I wave a dismissive hand at her and smile. "I'll come back. But you really shouldn't speak of this." She smirks. Giving me a look of knowing. "Child, I'm not speaking of a thing. I'm only thinking about what a shame it is that maintenance still hasn't fixed the lock on the back door." She turns and walks away from me. With one last request. "Room 509 Friday. Larry has been dying to meet you."

CHAPTER 3: MEET THE NIGHTINGALE

On the 3 am subway ride back into downtown Atlanta, I can't stop thinking about the bravery of my new nurse friend. I'm not usually impressed by humans. Most of them are quite selfish and boring. They all think they are not, but trust me, as someone who looks nineteen and is considered beautiful, I get a wide range of behavior thrown my way. Most of the time that ends in tears. Sometimes death.

I'm alone. Staring out the blurry window at the few city lights passing by. Or I suppose I'm the one passing. The lights are still. The Aquarium is lit in blue. It's pretty. Calming. The train rattles to a stop. On the opposing track, a train in the other direction. I peer inside the window. There is another lost soul. At this crazy hour. She's young. Her wiry curls bounce as she pops in her headphones. A bike next to her and a very bright, yellow raincoat. Modern fashion is strange. As my train rattles to life, she raises her head and looks at me. Our eyes meet and stay glued to each other as my train leaves her behind. Increasing the distance between the stranger and me.

Something sparks within me. I can't tell you why, but I want to see the shape of her almond eyes closer. And why not? I'm not in a rush. I have all the time in the world. I pull the emergency brake and the train startles to an abrupt stop mid-tunnel. I can hear the driver shouting. Inquiring whether there is an emergency. I mean, there is. I have to check just how the rain behaves in the stranger's hair.

Before the train driver can even reach my cart, I've pulled the doors open without much struggle. Yes, strength is an advantage of my condition. I slip into the tunnel, none of my steps making a sound and I look back. The lights of the other train are just fading ahead. If I hurry, I can catch it. But better yet, I'll catch HER at the main station. I think I know where she's going. Must be 'Five points.' That's where the lines connect. I step onto the platform and burst up the stairs into the city.

Cold air hits me, as I let my feet fly over the wet stone. A few cars still shine their lights, reflected in puddles across the ways. I scurry between them, so fast, they just see a shadow. I round a corner and hurl myself up a fire escape. The air smells already cleaner. No garbage, no unwashed humans to pollute it. I take a running leap and jump from one roof to the next. The illuminated skyline a nice decoration to my haste.

I can see the building. Fluorescent lights emanate through the windows, giving the surroundings a bit of a clinical feel. Just a general note, those lights need to go. There is nothing great about them. We had candles and everything looked a lot more romantic. The food, the people, the dirty streets, and death. In fluorescent ambiance, everything just looks sickly.

I hop down, knees barely bending. Four stories down, not a scratch. I could be flashy and backflip, landing like one of your cherished superheroes, but I'm not a show-off. And I'm in a hurry. I hope she's actually at the station. What if she got off a stop earlier? I discard the thought and rush the last yards towards the station, entering just like any of you would. Hood over my long hair, shoulders hunched in and walking briskly.

The two resident gargoyles judge me and everyone else equally. They don't like the lighting either. They both grimace down at me in utter discontent. Sorry buddies. I make my way down to the platform. A handful of people are just exiting a train. I scan them with immortal efficiency. By that I mean, I can smell things on you. Fear, sickness, arousal. It's usually not a very good cocktail, because you humans are so utterly bashful about

24

any and all of them, and pretend none of them exist. And when you do that, you make any of them more intense.

The passengers hurry off. None have almond eyes. Behind me, another train approaches and screeches to a halt. Smelling vaguely of urine. I slightly choke up. Disgusting. Only two people exit before it heaves itself back into motion. Did I miss her? I look around. Did she get off at the last stop? Oh no.

And then it hits me. A very faint scent of lilac and amber. Soft. Pleasant. Like candlelight. I take another breath and turn. From behind a big pillar, she steps out, pushing her bike. Her skin is smooth and impossibly soft. Her fingers long and elegant. Her eyes dart up to focus on the escalators and for a second they pass by me. Those darling, almond eyes. Rich in brown and musical in shape. I'm struck, but I turn quickly. She shouldn't see me staring at her so blatantly.

As she passes me, only inches away, her warm scent hits my nostrils again, making up for all the vile ones of the night. She's a nightingale. A fragile, beautiful songbird in a world of darkness. You see, a nightingale is an amazing creature. Sings songs most beautiful to attract a mate, but what it also summons are predators, enthralled by the impossibility of owning and devouring it. That's me, I suppose. A hawk, ready to hunt.

My heart skips a beat. I didn't know it could still do that. What a vulnerable feeling. I watch her ascend the escalator, struggling to keep her bike steady. I slow my thoughts down. Poetry helps.

Last night upon the stair,
I saw a girl who wasn't there.
She wasn't there again today.
Oh, how I wish she'd go away.

25

She loves a songbird, pure and fare.
A nightingale, a song of air.
Of Innocence, of life and yearning.
A bird of love, but dead come morning.

I always loved spinning poems further. Seeing if I can keep the cadence alive. Enough waiting. I let myself move into action and follow my nightingale up. She too looks at the gargoyles. She huffs a laugh. A bright sound. It seems to give her a shine.
The glow of the oncoming morning mixes with the fog. Different degrees of grey douse the city in coolness. Her bright yellow raincoat makes her stand out starkly. Like a first tulip through the snow. She mounts her bike and rolls through the streets. I can freely follow.

Then she stops. So do I. A few paces behind. But maybe not far enough? Her heartbeat quickens and she glances over her shoulder. She can't see me. But she must somehow know I'm following her. Attentive.

And just then, the clouds open and a stray bit of sunlight hits me. "Son of a mother!" I exclaim loudly and before my nightingale can turn fully, to look at the danger behind her, I've dissolved into nothing but thin air.

CHAPTER 4: A REGULAR PHONE CALL

Sunshine. The thing that sometimes slips my mind when I'm really focused on something. You see, it also doesn't kill me. But like so many other things, it's incredibly inconvenient. I sort of disappear and then reappear in the same spot when the sun goes down. I don't know why. I have no control over it. When my father gave me this infliction, so save me by the way, he didn't have time to explain the rules to me. So for centuries, I've had joyous moments if discovery. This particular one really surprised me.

But today I am lucky. About an hour ago, my nightingale came out just as I reappeared in the shadows across the street. She looked beautiful. Hair twisted together loosely. Strains thriving for freedom here and there. To no one's surprise, I have since been following her. Back to the trains, back to a different part of town. The infamous Peach-tree street. Oh, isn't it the most southern Georgia name you've ever heard?

I watched her go inside a building, all the others have left and she's in some sort of office. With very little snooping, it was listed on the mailbox by the floor, and I found, that my nightingale works at a place called 'Lifeline' a suicide hotline. I'm still chuckling to myself, here on the roof across from her. Out of all the places, she works at one dealing with the chronically depressed. We fit so well together. A match made in heaven, or the subway. Potatoe - potatoe if you ask me. But we've already established that you probably shouldn't.

Now, with the stolen phone from my early night's snack, I'm sitting here debating my options. Should I do the very human thing and call her? And what? Ask her out at her place of work? That just seems a tad unprofessional. Don't you think? I shake my head at myself. I'm an immortal and I still end up in the same predicaments most humans do. So I pick up the phone and dial.

Ring. Well, the phone works. Great. Another ring. Another. My eyebrow rises. Just the right one. For a suicide hotline, they sure make callers feel a bit rejected. I'll make a mental note to suggest changing that and save more lives. Then it clicks. I hold my breath.

"Suicide prevention hotline, Hello?" There is that bright voice. I smile. I could listen to it forever. "I didn't think anyone was gonna pick up." I hear myself saying, probably sounding flatly idiotic.

With that warmth, she replies: "It's what we're here for. Before we start, can I ask you whether you're currently in a safe place?"

I'm startled and actually look around me. Um, no. I'm on a roof eight stories up, looking into your window, while one of my legs dangles over the edge on a windy night. But of course, it's not what I tell my nightingale. "Sure." I reply, trying my best to sound convincing. I didn't actually think about this. Well, what's the worst that can happen? She'll track this stolen phone and I'll be long gone.

"Are you comfortable enough to talk?" Her voice has a velvety quality. It's beautiful. Without answering her question, I wonder: "What's your name?". That way I might be able to name my bird of wonder. She's startled. Shit. I should have answered her silly question first. This girl has more of a plan for this conversation than I do. "Vanessa, Ness for short."

Ness. I like the sound of the s. "Well Vanessa, Ness for short, I'm calling because I don't quite know what else to do." I hear the words come out of my mouth, still no plan where to go with this. But Ness is a professional. She tells me: "We get a lot of callers who feel like they have no way out, other than to end their own life - "I interrupt her with some actual frustration. "See, but that's just the problem for me. I'm immortal." Pause.

The pause continues. What am I doing? "You're immortal?" She asks gingerly, probably thinking I'm a complete nut-job. I nod. "I'm afraid so." Another pause. Has she pressed the 'call police and or asylum' button yet? "How do you know?" I frown. What's the harm, right? So I answer, quite honestly.
"I've been around for a few hundred years. So I'd say I'm pretty fucking certain. After a couple of decades, you kinda get this nagging feeling."

She laughs. I love that sound. It's free. But she stops herself, flustered, and apologizes. "I never laugh at callers. I'm genuinely sorry. Why don't you want to live anymore?" All I can think about is making her laugh again. Hear that sound again. "I'm what you would call a vampire." I can't believe I'm saying these things out loud. She takes a beat and then asks with some honesty: "Like, you eat people?"
"Not all parts, obviously. We focus on blood. I thought that was a pretty well-known fact." There it is again, her laugh. My own mouth curves up in a smile. Exposing my teeth. "You don't get to laugh often, do you?" I genuinely want to know.

Ness' velvet voice chirps back at me. "I work at a suicide hotline. Usually, when you speak with someone who's about to pull the trigger, laughter isn't a very helpful reaction." I look at her through the window. Her hair comes free of its confinement. "I can promise you, I've tried dying and laughter isn't going to do the trick." I watch her hold her mouth shut with her hand. I smirk. She's trying so hard to remain professional. I want to tease another laugh out of her.

"So you're the expert on this, how do I die?" Her body tenses up. "We try to save lives here, we don't exactly have a Rolodex of hitman at hand." I mumble, unable to help myself: "Trust me, most hitmen and hitwomen aren't very good at their job." There it is. A burst of a chuckle. "This is absurd," she says. You tell me, nightingale. It sure is. Then she asks: What else have you tried?"

Should I give her more honesty? I mean, at this point, what do I have to lose. "Today I tried to hang myself, but I got bored. First I saw the garbage truck coming, then I saw the wall. Then I saw the garbage truck leaving. Then I saw the wall again. Then I saw the school bus, wall. Then a kid running after the school bus, noticed the wallpaper was peeling off in the upper corner. After about an hour or so, I just couldn't take it anymore. So I got up and tore all the crappy paper off and that felt ok." I can see her grinning, trying to control herself and covering her face with her hands. I love her flustered. That's my reward for honesty.
"You're really-" "Messed up." I finish for her. Keeping her professional integrity intact. I'm chivalrous like that.

"What about you? Ever tried to kill yourself?" She goes quiet and I watch her rub her for-head. I hit a nerve. So I continue, "Your job is to establish trust with your callers, is it not?" I try to be playful, but her tone is colder. "My job is to listen and talk them off the edge." Fair enough. "And how can you do that if you don't know what the edge feels like?" Silence.

I've pushed her too far. Show my shot. Now I just have to kill her. Damn it. Then she says softly: "I haven't wanted to die, but my dad did." Daddy issues. Always a tough subject. Trust me. I have experience. She goes on, "We were at home. Just him and I. My mom was at work. She worked a lot when I was younger. And he'd been bad for a long time. Pancreatic cancer. Couldn't keep food down anymore. I used to make him soup thinking some chicken broth would heal it all. But it didn't. He tried a

30

few times. To eat it. Keep it down long enough for me. But the day he did it, he threw up in front of me, and I just asked him whether I made it wrong. He couldn't calm me down. I Just thought it was my fault. I thought I needed the soup to be just right, you know? That night he just put a plastic bag over his head and held it tightly until it was over." More silence. Different this time.

"Just like that?" I state more than ask. She nods and wipes a tear from her soft cheek. "Just like that. CVS bag. So unimportant, so normal. And I know he would have died anyway. But this. The willpower that must have taken. I'm still so mad at him. For wanting to not spend another moment with me so badly, he had to hold a plastic bag tightly enough to die." She's deeper than I thought. Gorgeous. "Then I guess you're messed up too." She smiles. A huff of air audible. "I'm trying to use it to help others. I guess it does sometimes. Sometimes suicide seems to be the only way out for people." She looks my way. Rain obscuring me. But I know she's spotted at least a figure over on the other roof.

I smile. A plan emerges in my brain. "I don't think you're supposed to advocate for it." I get another small huff. "How many times have you tried?" Perfect opening for me. "Tonight? Twice. I give it a moment each time, to see if it works. You know?" I can see Ness shaking her head. Her beautiful, curly hair swaying just a split second later. "And when it doesn't work?" I grin. She played right into my hand.
"Then I try again." I hang up. She startles. Looks at the phone with halted breath. Fuck.
She looks my way. Her inhales get quicker. She looks directly at me as I complete my little show and let myself plunge off the roof to the echo of her muffled scream.

CHAPTER 5: FRIENDS WITH DEATH

It was a bit of an unfair move. Setting her up like that. My way of flirting might be a tad...unusual. But damn effective. I stand in the alley hiding in the shadows as she tries to explain our little soiree to the EMT and the firefighters. No, Vanessa, Ness for short, there indeed is no body. No, you didn't imagine it. And yes, every word I told you was the crazy truth.

I watch the rescue team leave her in the rainy night. She looks around again. Into the alley, I occupy. I smile at her openly, knowing her human eyes can't make me out. But she must feel me. Her scent changes. Flickering little candlelight. She'll be my nightingale. A hunt of a different kind. I want her. I want her to invite me into her life. To have a choice and choose me.

Maybe I'll postpone my little date with death. He doesn't seem too eager to show up on time anyway. Maybe I'll have one last adventure with life. See it through her eyes. Ask her what her heart feels like, when like now, it skips a beat. Excitement. I bite my lip in anticipation. This, dear reader, is going to be fun. I cordially invite you to witness the death of the nightingale.

Most sincerely,

The Hawk

CHAPTER 6: THE OTHER SIDE - NESS

It's strangely cold today. I don't even feel bad fully indulging in my tea addiction. Peppermint with a dash of lemon all night long. You'd think that during the night shift, I'd be drinking coffee, like most people. But I actually don't like coffee. It's bitter. I never got it.
So I wait for the water heater to do its job. It's taking its sweet time. The new kid stares at me and we do that awkward, tight-lipped eyebrow-raise thing that is a copout for not knowing what words to pick. Like, yeah I can't believe that it takes an entire 4,35 minutes for this thing to boil water either. Or right? Tea. Mhm. So many things we could say here, that all say absolutely nothing at all.

But genuinely, he should have some manners. When you just started a job you don't hog the office coffee maker or tea kettle. You wait your turn. That's just common sense to me. New kid, his actual name being Thomas Newman... No I didn't make that up, looks like he's twelve. There's a bit of fuzz on his upper lip that looks like two-day-old sour-dough starter. He proudly told me earlier that he's trying to grow a beard in. Good luck, buddy. It'll be a while.

And now Thomas yawns. What a newb. This is the night shift, honey. Get out while you still can. Thinking about having to teach this child makes me want to roll my eyes. But I do, in fact, have manners and even let him fill his tea up first. I don't think my slight annoyance shows.

"Ness!" Matt croaks my name from the other word like a magical summons. "Coming." I reply, although judging by how slowly little Thomas pours his tea like he's creating a Picasso, I'm not actually certain when that will be. "You have Emma on the line."

35

Ok, time to hurry up. I take Thomas's slightly shaking hand and finish his tea for him before I pour my own. "Sorry," I explain. "But we're a suicide hotline. If we don't pick up on time people lose their trust in us."

And that's true. Lifeline has been around for almost a decade, but I really whipped it into shape four years ago when I started creating a protocol of rules to abide by. All callers go through training, but there are just some things that help more than others. Those you only understand with experience, which sadly, I have.

I rush to the other room and sit down in front of the screen. Everything is on Zoom these days. Even some of our suicide calls. I press the button and the screen shines to life. "There she is. My nightly favorite." I chime with familiarity. Emma is one of my regular callers. She started to call and immediately hung up eighteen months ago when she was still a he. Her words. Not mine. Today she looks worse for the wear. A big shiner on her cheek. Next to me, Thomas gasps, and I want to smack him like a horsefly. Empathy is good. Pity is not.

"Hey, Ness." I smile at her. I've been told it's reassuring. "I waited all day until you got to the office. Sorry. I needed to call. I'm so sorry." I shake my head, hand on my chest. Calm and slow. One step at a time. The rules that I wrote are on the board in front of me. "No need to apologize. Bad day?" The poor girl doesn't have to nod. Tears sprout from her eyes and drip heavily down her pretty cheeks. She's a stunner, but somehow she doesn't know it. Gorgeous big eyes and lashes I've always been a bit jealous of. Top and bottom. "Your dad again?" I ask gingerly and more tears rush out.
"He told me I can't go to Thanksgiving like this. It would be embarrassing. I should just kill myself. It would be easier for everyone. He said he doesn't know what he did to cause this defect in his 'son'." Another audible gulp from Newman behind me and I'm half tempted to scold

him right there. I breathe with Emma. Calmly. Not averting my eyes. Being perfectly present with her. Then I ask, "You know where his reaction comes from, right?" She nods. "Fear."

I nod. Mad at her father, mad at a world where a teen can't become themselves on their own terms. "And you know that has nothing to do with you, right?" Emma nods again. We've talked through this a few times. But talking and day-to-day life can be starkly different. "Thank you." She huffs.

"No need. Is he hurting you again?" I take my time with this next part. "Do you want to report it? Or do you want me to?" I can see her breath hitching as she violently shakes her head. True fear. "No! That would blow up the family and everyone would just blame me, and then he was right all along. You know?" Oh, the argument of the self-fulfilling prophecy. I wish parents would visit us once a month and see what kind of pressure they put their children under and what it does to them. Especially teens. How many suicides and attempts could be avoided through communication and less fear? It seems so very simple. And yet...

I've always been great at relating to my callers. I'm young, barely in my twenties, so I understand most of the immediate questions and concerns. But also, because of my dad. I know we all have 'Daddy issues' but for me, it wasn't anything like that when he was around, it was about how he left. He was a wonderful father. Kind, funny, playful. Before we moved and repainted the old house, he and I had a day of hide-and-seek paintball. It was the most fun I've ever had. Splotches of color everywhere. It took two months before I picked the last of the yellow, shiny speckles out of my curls. They were still reflecting the sunlight during his funeral.
It was his suicide that marked me. I wanted to help others avoid this fate and avoid what that leaves behind. That

feeling of the person not wanting another moment with you.

That pang of pain and that anger and grief. The weird details that stick with you of their way out, instead of their life and moments with you. When I now think of my father, the first thoughts aren't chasing him with my paintball gun. They are the fact that I was in the next room when he took his life. They are that the receipt of the cough drops I bought him was still in the plastic bag he used to take his life.

So I dedicated my life to working here. Lifeline. I've done amazingly. Our numbers are wonderful. Every EMT and Firefighter knows each of our names and they adore us. The pay is pretty shitty, but luckily my mom is a doctor and we're solid. We're not great. But we'll be ok.

"Emma? I can report him for you. We can place you in a shelter for a while." Emma thinks. Heavy. "I'll be ok tonight. Promise." Believe them at face value. The rule in front of me shines right into my view. I nod. "Check-in call tomorrow?" I ask. It's our little ritual. She agrees. Wipes her tears and I get a small smirk. She looks at my tea. "Did you forget the milk today?" She's very attentive and correct. I like my tea with a little bit of milk. Like a nice London Fog, but with Peppermint. I can't help myself and glance quickly at Newb-mustache-in progress and tell her: "I was in a rush." She smiles. That's great. "See you tomorrow." And the screen fades to black.

CHAPTER 7: ARE THE GARGOYLES WATCHING?

When I leave the office it's late. Or early. A matter of perspective. But I'm so used to working this shift, I like the night. Especially right now, in the fall. It's raining. Actually, it's pelting down. Which makes the streets reflect each glowing light in a neon-colored carpet. It looks like the end result of my dad and my paintball fest.

My bright yellow raincoat makes me look like a Chornobyl mushroom. But I'd rather stick out as a fashion disaster than get hit by some idiot, who can't see me at night. There are always plenty of them out on the streets. I roll on my bike and though I avoid the puddles, I enjoy the drive. It's peaceful. Blurry lights all around me. I can jump from the sidewalks on the streets in the middle of downtown and no one cares. The night is wonderful. It's my playground.

I hop off at the station and shoulder the bike. It's always heavy and I'm sure I'm doing damage to my body in the long run. The station is empty. Some remnant mud graces the floor. The platform smells mossy. Not in a good way. I hurtle the bike onto the standstill train. I'm alone, so I have options. I sit. It feels good. Even though the seats are hard under the thin layer of grey padding. The train rattles into motion. Without thought, I pop in my headphones and listen to my favorite podcast. It's a morbid one. Feel free to judge. I have this theory, that if you've been through some serious trauma, you prefer people and art that reflects that. So I listen to murder. It relaxes me.

The city blurs by. Hey Atlanta. You neo-noir blanket of fog, I barely see in the daylight. I look up as the train stops at the next station. Above ground this time. Another train on the rails across. Movement catches my eye. I've always wanted hair like that. One always wants the opposite, right? Blond, long, silky hair. And the bluest eyes I've ever seen. Piercing. Startling. A shiver runs through me. The train starts again and those eyes blink at me one last time. I shiver again. What is that intensity?

Gone. More darkness engulfs my wagon in another tunnel. RATTLE. RATTLE. RATTLE. The thought of those eyes. Ice blue. Really ice blue. So unique. For the next few stations, I listen to a story about a California serial killer in the '60s. They're somehow always from California...Why? You don't have to kill people. Go to the beach. Enjoy the sunshine. But while the story moves along, station after station, my mind drifts back to those haunting eyes telling a tale of depth I've never seen before.

I get onto the platform. I have to switch trains. A few old, rusted columns make me turn and guide my bike funny. I have to stop and pull the stand back up. I always, ALWAYS hit my ankle on that thing at least once per day. When I continue walking something is different. I feel that chill again. I look around, but nothing. Just that chill. I close my eyes and try to shake it off. But the image of ice-blue eyes comes to mind and creeps that chill across my entire body. Like a nail up my spine. It's strange. Beautiful, scary, haunting.

The two local gargoyles hang and ponder about the meaning of life in the main hall. Like they always do. I stick my tongue out a little. And I could swear one of them blinks at the insult. I call them Pinky & Brain. Like their namesakes, these guys are stationary and plotting. All the time. I wish I could decorate them for Christmas. They'd look a lot friendlier with a Santa hat.

Outside, the night starts to give way to the creeping dawn. Fog, grey and thick. I just push the bike the last little bit. That feeling of strangeness doesn't leave me. My heart beats so loudly, that I feel it in my throat. It's just such an odd thought. There's no one there. I know it. But I listen into the misty air. Raindrops that have puddled on a roof, finally splotch down. A lonely siren far away. A car on the wet street and a screeching dove. But what I don't hear, are footsteps. Why do I feel like there's someone behind me? The clouds desperately want to open to a single ray of sunshine. That's when I risk one little glance over my shoulder. Is there another person? Is that strange, strange feeling rooted in more than my tired state of mind? Then I hear a curse. Muffled, but clearly spoken.

So as the sun indeed illuminates this moody morning, I dare a look back. And there it is. Absolutely nothing but more fog. A few glittery dust particles dance in the wind and I wonder what harmful chemical plants polluted our air. I'm losing my remaining marbles. Clearly. There is no one following me. I continue up the steps to my house. Somehow that scary, lovely chill is gone.

CHAPTER 8: THE PERFECT LIFE

"Not another step." My wonderful mother practically yelps and me and my bike freeze mid-motion. Normal people get a hello, or at this hour of the early morning, some peace. I get a yelp. Thanks, Mom. She waves her tiny hands through the air at my shoes. "They soak my carpet." ...Our carpet. My eyebrows rise in protest, but before a single word can possibly pass my lips, she continues. "So does the rest of you. Take those silly clothes off."

I manage to at least close the door behind me and lean the bike against the rack we installed. "Mom, I'm just getting in." Not that that is a strong enough reason for my mother to cut me some slack. "And we just made tea. But you're not getting any unless you stop dripping mud all over the place." I know the woman out-stubborns me by a long shot. I don't know why I still put up a fight. "Mother, it's five in the morning. Who the hell is we?"

Before I can fully take my bright raincoat off, to my mother's judgmental eye-roll, a chiseled, beautiful face pops around the corner, tea already extended towards me, grinning with that mischievous smile that completely disarms me every time I get to see it. Luke, my handsome, smart, and kind boyfriend of three years. He was there through the worst of it and is practically already family. We met when I was still eighteen and became a mixture of best friends, lovers, family, and all the other good things. He's a bit older, finished graduate school early, and researches crazy things I cannot wrap my mind around. Everyone knows we'll get married someday. I just kept pushing off a possible engagement since my dad died. It didn't feel right. I remember Luke being so wonderfully traditional and asking my father for permission to propose. My heart jumped with glee. I've never had butterflies that wild. I was so giddy.

And then I was mad at my dad. He didn't deny him. He gave him his blessing and told him he loved him very much, but he sat me down and had a talk with me. A

TALK. About true happiness and that he'd love for me to truly get to know myself first. Maybe make a few mistakes. Maybe get my heart broken once and really know what marriage means. I felt very confused at that moment. I remember asking him why he couldn't just let me marry the love of my life and him telling me that I don't know life yet. It was not my favorite 'father-daughter' moment.

But the thoughts pass through me as I hook the raincoat and try to fish the teacup from Luke's strong hands. He has the audacity to retract the steaming tea like a cat toy. "You might want to switch pants too." He winks at me. It's sexy, so I can't really get mad, but it's also annoying. I look at my pants. They might be a tad moist-ish. "I don't like you two hanging out alone. You conspire behind my back." I say to both of them as they sheepishly block the kitchen entrance from me, shoulder to shoulder, like weird linebackers.

My mom does her best impression of an innocent face. "Darlin, we would never dare." Yeah, right you wouldn't. Psh.

"Nope. Never" Luke backs her up. What is this weird conspiracy? I look from one to the other. Then to that beautiful, hot, aromatic cup of tea. Somehow it makes my icy toes bite just a little bit more. They're mean. I attempt a step and they shove closer together. Definitely determined not to let me pass. What is this? The caves of Moria? My mom grins and looks at my legs. "Pants, my love." Unbelievable.

My face gives away my thoughts about this beautiful moment because Luke chimes: "Your daughter is really cute, when

she gets mad." - Now I'll definitely say no when he proposes. I have principles. My mom angles her head and now she reminds me of a dodo. "Bless her heart", it's really the Southern version of "Go eff yourself". Just so we're clear. "You better keep up the training when you two get married." Now my glare actually has a bit of bite to it. She clocks it. But I oblige and take off the pants. As

44

I turn, ready to go, my mom is about to start, looking at my hoodie. I throw my hands up and tell her: "It's this or I'm coming in naked. Move." And finally. I get tea and kitchen access.

As I strut past them, pant-less, but with an enormous amount of dignity, Luke pokes my butt cheek. Above the sweater, since mom is present, but I still don't like it. I've told him many times and I don't understand how he's not hearing me. Sometimes he does that. He doesn't really hear me. But the thoughts of the cracks in the paint, so to say, all vanish at the side of what's on the stove. Those two conspirators made me breakfast for dinner. I squeal. It's my favorite. Eggs and bacon. Crispy. I sigh. True pleasure. I wolf down a few bits and remember: "Aren't you working today? Tomorrow or whatever it is?" Luke's eyes sparkle. "Thoughts I'd stop by to watch you devour an exorbitant amount of bacon before I head in." I grin at him, still chewing. So classy.

"Did you bring your aliens home again?" Now it's his turn to glare at me. He hates it when I make his serious research cute. "They're jellyfish. Not aliens. Though the resemblance is uncanny."

Mom, the ever-positive cheerleader, steps up to the table and grabs a printout of one of those aliens. "Did he tell you that they got a new one? 900 years old and immortal." I squint at the wiggly creature I'm being presented with. "

"How do you know it's immortal and not just really old and wrinkly." I ask and get a head tilt from Luke. But today he plays. Nice. "We named him Socrates. And no wrinkles. Whenever a part of him dies, he grows it back. Arms, organs, brain. So we're really close." His expectant expression is so childlike. "You're close to finding true immortality?" He nods. Excited that I get it. "But if you're an immortal jellyfish, what do you do all day? Sounds super boring." His face changes, actually considering my words. "It might be. The other two we found that aren't quite as old, both tried to commit suicide." I have so many questions. But before I can ask, he answers. "They tried to jump into the neighboring tank that had carnivorous fish in it. They wanted to be eaten." Well, all I can think of is: "Tell them to give me a call sometime. I work the night shift." I return that wink and shove another piece of bacon into my mouth.

He kisses my cheek and collects all of his alien papers. "Have to head in."

"Don't let Socrates die on your watch."

"Put some pants on, wifey."

And then he's off solving the mysteries of life and death. I sigh as the front door falls into the lock. I love him. I really do. But I feel like I always have to be 'on' with him. That gets a little bit exhausting over time. Sometimes I don't want to fit into that box, he thinks I belong.

My mom ogles after him. She adores him. "When are you gonna marry that boy?"

My mom ogles after him. She adores him. "When are you gonna marry that boy?"

I nearly drop the bacon. She has no subtlety.

"I think, it's traditional for him to ask first." I fire back, sounding more annoyed than she deserves. But despite my tone, Mom digs deeper.

"He's perfect for you. Great family, a solid job, and he loves you more than he loves himself. You know how rare that is?"

I do, in fact, know how rare that is. I also know I should be jumping up and down with glee. But Dad's thoughts are stuck in my head. "Take your time. Know yourself first. Understand what you need for true happiness." Deep down I know I got mad at him because he had a point. I didn't get to tell him that he was right. That I appreciate him protecting me from rushing things. But he was.

I look at my mom and scowl. "Why don't you marry him?"

Her eyebrows bunch in worry. Asking without words. She was never able to hide a single thought. "I just don't understand what you're so afraid of. He's all you ever wanted."

I'm afraid of this happily ever after. I am. If I get it, then what? Then it can only fall apart, right? Now, or in twenty years. Every morning I would worry. Is today the day my perfect world crumbles to dust? It gives me anxiety. What if he died? What if I died? And then the other will live only halfway? With a constant broken heart? Like my wonderful, pure mother?

After Dad, she didn't even consider dating or fully coming back to life. She's been a shadow of herself. She's there for me and work. That's it. The two other pieces. But she's still young, and beautiful. But dim.

She used to light up any room she walked into. Her bright laugh was intoxicating. Every friend I brought over would love my mother and want to move in. And the way my dad looked at her? Like he was the luckiest man on the planet. Always in disbelief that he actually got to marry her, the love of his life. Now if she smiles, it doesn't reach her eyes. It's like two different faces. Her eyes look tired. Like she still cries herself to sleep. And then she puts on a friendly mask for me, encouraging me to seek out my own perfect life. It scares me half to death.

Mom looks at me. Sometimes I think she can read my thoughts.

"He would have wanted you to be happy, you know?" I do know that. But somehow being happy would also feel like a betrayal. To her, to him, to me. A good psychiatrist could make a ton of money off of me.

"I'm going to bed." I state. "Was a long night."

Mom tries one more time. Padding my arm in that 'loving. mother way'. "I'm sorry, it's just...Don't let life's best moments pass you by."

Our eyes connect and I can't take the depth of that moment. All of her pain is visible in a single glance.

I kiss her cheek. "Good night, Mother. Please stop being a pain in my butt."

47

I hear her smile forming. That half smile that won't ever reach her eyes again and make her nose crinkle. "I can't see that happening, darling."
"Neither can I."
And I leave the heaviness of the kitchen behind.

CHAPTER 9: WHAT HAPPENS IN A DREAM

My eyes fall shut so quickly, that I am unsure whether I took both socks off. Dreamland takes me away. Soothing. And then there is a delicate finger tracing my earlobe. A light scratch. The kind that traces shivers down your spine and makes the peach fuzz on your neck stand up.
A sigh parts my lips and I can feel the slight rush of air even asleep.
The next vivid image is of interlaced fingers. Squeezing in unison and ecstasy. Hands writhing in their own form of love-making.
As a long, sharp nail impales delicate skin, blood sprouts. Freely into a voluptuous, full droplet. Beautiful. A pair of lips nears it. Excruciatingly slow. A tongue teasing a slow circle around the small hurt. Finally dipping in and licking off the redness. Only clean skin remains.
Another sigh. Entirely out of my control. The barrier between the reality of my own body and dreamland has been washed away. My wrist, fragile and feminine is near that sinful mouth. A pair of elongated canines gently scraping it. Enjoying the small pale lines they leave behind.
Marking my skin. A long strand of golden hair falls and brushes against me. So soft.
I turn over in my sleep. Sweating and tightening my muscles, without my knowledge or any remnants of control.
A thumb parts my own lips with such a confident sense of ownership. Its nail scrapes against my skin ever so slightly. In my dream, I slightly suck on it as it departs. Tasting the salty skin. Wanting more. So much more.
I toss again, I think. The taste of her skin. Like fresh rain. But cold. And then I see her eyes. The iciest blue. Unnerving. As they connect with my own, they turn silver. Like liquid, cold night.
I wake up and sit up straight. My heart pounds. I'm drenched in sweat. Those eyes. Those haunting, terrifying eyes.

CHAPTER 10: WHEN DEATH CALLS I ANSWER

Sure enough. I wake up with my socks still on. Sexy.
Nodding at myself in approval, I slowly rise. It's late afternoon and the light outside is already dimming. Really there was not much light to begin with. I could hear the rain pummeling the window with unrelenting fervor. Like a constant knock.

My shirt is sweat through. Drenched. The dream was so vivid, that I still feel the slight rush of adrenaline making my cheeks blush and my blood rise to the apex of my thighs. I shake off the thought. Those eyes.

I twist my hair into my go-to style. I call it the "lazy birds nest" and throw on some jeans and a sweater. I know I'll have to hop back into the rain jacket, so what's the point in being fashionable? I work at night, mostly alone.

Downstairs is empty. Mom is probably working at the hospital. She works a ton. I visited her once with my entire class for "bring your children to work day". They all wanted to see what a doctor does. It was fun at first. Seeing all the instruments and technical equipment.

Then my mother wanted to give us an advanced version of a nonsmoking lesson and took us to see a real lung in chlorophyll. I've never seen so many children puke at the same time. Me included. Although I just puked because I can't stand the smell when others do it. It was not a good day. And the kid's parents weren't amused either. I wasn't invited to any birthday parties for a good while. But on the bright side, I don't think many of my classmates ever touched a cigarette.

The kitchen feels cozy, even without my mom in it. I grab the lunch I prepped a few days ago and stuff it into my backpack. Out the door, I go.

The grey hits me. The softness engulfs me in a shrouded hug. Claiming. My rain jacket doesn't feel so bright anymore. Faded. Like the daylight. Just disappearing behind the houses across.

The thought of those eyes hits me again and I squint through the heavy rain. Something seems to be moving

51

in that alley. As I doubt my own sanity once again, I carry the bike down the steps and mount it. Even though the asphalt is slippery, I love riding in the rain. The sound the rubber makes through the water. That silvery rattle. Tiny, little splashes. I love the blurry lights that reflect everywhere too. And the lack of people who dare to come out and play. It takes a special kind of person to love this weather.

After my usual transit including subway stops, greeting Pinky and Brain, and avoiding an especially obnoxious driver, texting behind the wheel, I see our office building. It's pretty central. My guess is that the city thought, our cause is important enough to place us smack dab in the middle. Not that our location really matters, we don't do house calls. But I'm not complaining. I love driving by the Fox Theatre and its shiny lights. The restaurants around here are always filled with beautiful, trendy people, who care a lot more about their outfits than I do. As I roll through Peach Street, I see the dinner crowd. Diminished by the weather, but a few brave souls nonetheless.

In my favorite bar, the Edison, a very steampunk-inspired place with obvious lightbulb designs, there's a kissing couple in the window. He gently strokes her hair behind her ear and nuzzles the tip of her button nose. She smiles and leans into him. Cute. I shamelessly watch them as she opens her eyes and even from here, they appear bright, ice blue.

Like a bolt of lightning, the image surges through me and I swerve. Eyes back on the road. My heart skips a beat.

I hop off my bike and push the last few minutes. As I glance back, looking at the couple again I see her clearly. Her eyes are brown. Like my own. Whatever is going on with my head, it doesn't seem very safe.

I close the door behind me and peel the hood back from the jacket. I'm very likely losing my mind.

I struggle to hang the bike on the rack with my name tag. For some reason, it's one row up, which I've never quite understood since I'm one of two people biking here and the other person only works day shifts. But I have a weird affinity for following proper rules. It would feel like a bit of a rebellion to hang the bike wrong. Like I'm stealing someone else's spot.

The office is almost empty. Matt and the new kid are just putting on their jackets. Matt is the one who started it all. An age ago he went to school for political science and after graduating decided that this was the best way to actually make a difference. He told me in my hiring interview and I remember being both impressed and scared at what that meant.

"You cool if we leave five minutes early today? I gotta take Thomas to the station."

Thomas looks at me, feeling the need for further justification. I must look particularly scary today.

"It's raining pretty hard. I have a weak immune system."

...I'm sure he does.

"Yeah, no worries." I tell them both, feeling proud of my own power as I struggle with the zipper of my rain jacket. The damn thing is stuck and doesn't want to allow me even a tiny moment of gloating. I bike through any weather. Gloating should be an added benefit.

I just move on to the kitchen. Tea, my favorite thing after gloating. "Just give me one minute" I shout and push the button on the water kettle.

I select my favorite, a peach-mint mixture. Lovely for this weather and smells just heavenly. The phone RINGS.

"Matt, can you start this? I'll be right there."

I hang my jacket and prep my coup. Another RING and I hear the door fall into place downstairs. Damn it. RING. I take the kettle to pour the water but the cable sparks and gives me a little shock. What is happening today? I unplug the likely murderous machine and rush to the other room. RING.

"Suicide prevention hotline, Hello?"

A breath of surprise is on the other line.

"I didn't think anyone was gonna pick up."

Stupid tea addiction. Feels so silly. I sit down. My own poster of rules and guidelines stares back at me.

"Answer within the first two rings." I avert my eyes. My gaze goes to the roof across. Through the small waves of rain on the glass, I can spot a figure. I think. Maybe it's just a very strange chimney?

"It's what we're here for. Before we start, can I ask you whether you're currently in a safe place?"

That chimney just moved. It's definitely a person. If I close my eyes, will those beautiful, haunting blue eyes appear in my mind?

CHAPTER 11: THE REAL WORLD

The call ends so abruptly. It takes my breath away. One moment we banter back and forth. Dark and a little morbid, but it brought butterflies into my stomach. The next she makes me believe she'll die tonight and hangs up. I'm still reeling and cannot stop thinking about her. The clever sparing of words. It made me smile in a way I haven't in a very long time.

Immortal. Sure. It's silly and obviously fabricated. But it's also clever and exciting and new. A vampire. Her imagination made my night. I pictured a girl, with blue eyes and long, blonde hair with a cape and a red collar. Absurdly large fangs and a weird hissing sound. Vampire.

I wonder if she keeps up this game in other areas of her life or if it's just a wild coping mechanism. They teach us about those. As counselors. There are so many. People do all sorts of things to escape reality. I don't even blame them anymore. It's such a divisive world. If becoming a character in Dungeons and Dragons gets you through the day, great. If you believe your superpowers will kick in any second, amazing. I hope they are really cool ones. If you believe your intuition can summon the dead or your dreams tell you the future, all wonderful. The vampire thing is a new one to me though. So props for being unique.

I feel so bad for chuckling a few times. Despite my training and experience, somehow I couldn't keep a straight face. I hope that didn't set her off. But I don't think it did. Somehow while talking, she made ME open up. I think that surprised me the most. I haven't talked about Dad's death in a long time.

Ever. I don't talk about his death. I'm just mad at him. I stew in that feeling. And to be super honest, instead of getting therapy, I give it. Essentially. It's my very own form of reality escape. Talk about the good things he did. Avoid that day at all costs. Ignore his illness and his pain leading up to it and ignore my own pain about all of it.

So she's a vampire. Cool. I understand completely.

The thing I don't understand is her hanging up. She tells me sweetly that she'll "try again" and hangs up. It actually took me several seconds to understand what was happening and to follow my own protocol. When someone threatens to harm themselves or others in a call with us, we HAVE TO call the police. No exceptions.

So I did. I told them about the person I saw on the opposite roof and that I thought she was the caller. I told them I saw her fall.

And now I'm standing here, on the street with EMTs and a firetruck. Two police officers are as confused by my call as I am. There is no body. The street is wet and glistening. It's frigid and the air stings a little bit. Everyone is just a little bit grumpy to have to be out here.

"Are you sure you saw her jump?" The younger of the two officers ask me again and I tell him with conviction that yes, I saw someone spread their arms and let themselves fall.

"So not a jump." He clarifies.

Like that's the part we should get hung upon. Fall, jump, at about eight stories dead is dead.

"Maybe she just walked it off?" I offer, but I hear it sounding quite hollow as it's being spoken.

Our little, grumpy group collectively looks up. High up.

"Ma'am, that's highly unlikely." The older officer chimes in, trying to refrain from the word 'crazy' in his mind.

I nod. He's not wrong.

His radio chimes. It's the EMT who checked the slick roof.

"Sir, nobody up here. All clear."

Ah, ok. No one hiding up there either.

"You know, honey, with the rain coming down on the old windows like that, I'm sure it could've looked like some sort of figure."

He just 'honeyd' me and I don't appreciate it. I know he's trying to be sweet, but it feels condescending. But what's the point in saying anything?

"You always work the night shift?" The younger one asks.

"Most of the time."

"Maybe it would be good to switch it up. See some sunlight."

He pats my arm and I have no idea what to make of that gesture. Can I get arrested for swatting away a police officer? I don't swat but ruefully smile.

"Maybe." I say.

I look up again as they start to wrap up the show. Only heavy, full raindrops. No vampires are falling from the sky.

The older officer lingers before hopping into his car and asks one last time.

"Are you sure you are ok?"

"Yeah, I'll be fine. The morning shift has already arrived, I'll go home and sleep. All better tomorrow, right?"

He smiles with that caring, kind dad expression that reminds me of my own father. So sweet and sometimes so clueless.

They drive off and the night goes quiet again. Peaceful. Only the window lights reflect on the street.

And Kyle's moving shadow up in my office.

Kyle is on the morning shift and he came in early to cover me reporting this. Even he looks concerned. I really have lost my marbles. However many I had remaining.

With a heavy sigh, I mount my bike and slowly roll down the street. I barely glance down the alley, afraid to spot a shadow of a woman who isn't really there. Maybe they are right. Maybe I do need some sunshine.

CHAPTER 12: INTO THE BLUE

Obviously, I forgo the thought of sunshine. I thought about it for about a solid minute.

I bike across town. Not feeling the subway and stuffy train cars. I need the wind in my hair and the misty air in my face. Maybe it'll wake me up enough and shake me out of this dreamy mental fog.

It's early in the day. Late for me. About six in the morning. Spaghetti Junction, the worst traffic catastrophe anyone ever came up with, is already thrumming with bumper-to-bumper anger. Honking, inching, stopping. Happy Wednesday. I'm grateful for the bike.

After only about twenty minutes, I spot the aquarium. One of Atlanta's crown jewels. With good reason.

I swerve through the familiar parking lot, past the half-high gates to the entrance. I started feeling at home here. George, the nicest human on this planet saw me coming through the cameras about two minutes ago and buzzes the doors open. They both swing inwards and give me a chance at a grand entrance.

I take it. The lobby always feels wondrously inviting. It's like stepping into calm blue light. With the ceiling shapes coming down like giant, reflective jellyfish, I already feel like a diver. The balcony looks like a coral reef but is smooth and shiny.

"Is this early or late for you, kiddo?"

I smile. George is such a kind soul, he gets to call me kiddo.

"Both I think."

He takes my bike from me and stashes it behind the desk. He's been here forever. Since the place opened. So George is inventory. He belongs to the aquarium as the fish do.

"They're down in lab two," he tells me. But I know.

"Thanks, Georgi." I say and earn a playful scowl. I deserve one. The man is in his sixties.

I wonder through the empty lobby through the tunnel.

The tunnel. One of my favorite places in the world. Above and below it's an aquarium. So even at six in the morning, schools of bright fish lazily meander about. It's mesmerizing. A large, flat one swims a few steps with me. I think he's saying hello. Sometimes when I'm lucky, they get curious and swim right up to the glass. It's a funny, alienesque world. I love it. It's real, but it's not.

Then a large, all-consuming shadow covers all light from above.

My favorite. This is Taroko, the gentle giant.

Like the night sky, the spots on this whale shark make me gaze in awe. He's just beautiful. And he's giving me a slow twirl as he passes. What a show-off. He knows I'm a lady. My eyes follow him until he disappears into the depths of the largest aquarium in the world.

After the tunnel comes the small exhibit room with seahorses. As much as I'd like to see the little guys, it's not what I'm here for and I find the service door, that is so carefully hidden in the dark sides of the wall.

It clicks open and I stand in the elevator room. Strangely bright with fluorescent bulbs hovering above. A sign reads: "Don't enter with fins, shoes only."

One would think this is a joke, but some of the diving instructors and trainers don't care and waddle through the place in their fins. The splashing noise scares the sea lions. So they put up the sign. With A BING the door opens and without much thought I try to step inside, only to be surprised by a tall figure blocking my way.

My eyes flick to the security monitor in the corner. The image shows the empty elevator.

The tall, imposing figure steps out into the elevator room and my heart picks up several paces. Broad shoulders. I can't see the face. I make a wide birth around him. With a gentle, chivalrous reach, his hand holds the door for me. I step inside the elevator. I can hear my heartbeat in my throat. Who is that? At six in the morning?

I glance at his hand. Elegant. Clean nails. Slightly round. Not what I would expect from a man. A classic shirt sleeve. Jeweled buttons. As shiny as the fish. The hand drifts off with careful ease. That's not an employee here. Another look at the camera makes me doubt my sanity again. The room is empty. What?

BING!

The elevator door closes and I go down. My heart threatens to jump out of my chest. I try to calm my anxiety when another BING interrupts all thought. The door opens again. The lab.

Blue lights greet me. An odd place to be sure. Large aquariums on light tables. Jellyfish float and bubble in slow bulbs up and down.

A QUACK and I stop, letting a still fluffy, growing pair of penguin chicks pass by like they own the place. In all fairness, it is their home.

"That's a sight for sore eyes." Luke's voice breaks my thoughts and I brighten up. I point at the little bird chicks and ask him, "You just let them run amok?"

He grins giving his dimples a chance to make me swoon a bit.

"They like riding the elevator."

He kisses me and I feel better. He's my safe place.

The penguin exhibit here is one of my favorites. Especially because they do let the chicks run around until they can join their parents up top. They're quite noisy and very opinionated. QUACK. I hear behind me as I follow Luke into his office.

We pass by several tanks of various jellyfish. Beautiful and otherworldly. He takes my hand. Damp. Is he a bit nervous? He eyes me as he leads me to a big, centered tank.

"Vanessa, meet Socrates. Socrates, meet the love of my life."

With all of his excitement, he squeezes me like a stuffed animal and pokes me in the side, which tickles but isn't fun. I roll my eyes at him and huff a little annoyed.

"What?" He dares to ask.

I wrap my hands around my waist as he tries to playfully poke me again. Why does he not listen to me?

61

"You know, I don't like it when you do that."
He sighs in that 'no big deal'-fashion. It's charming, but it drives me crazy too.
"Don't be so sensitive. You're mine. I get to poke you."
Men and ownership. I swear we need to start distributing bonsai trees to every male. To get the territory marking out of the way and under control.
I let it go. Hard to explain. Much more importantly, I stare ahead at this tank. A stunning, electrifying creature contracts and releases his way through the water. Little sparkles all over his hide. I place my hand against the glass and the creature extends a tentacle. Electricity sparks and shocks me. I can feel a little jolt. I'm stunned.
"He likes you." Luke purrs into my ear.
"What was that?"
He smirks and whispers into my ear, making the hair on my neck stand up with his hot breath.
"It's how he kills his prey."
I retract my hand. Fascinated. A little intimidated. Turned on my Luke's whisper. So many mixed thoughts. I focus on Socrates, the murderous jellyfish.
"And he's immortal? You can't kill him?"
"Nothing is truly immortal, but he can regenerate." Luke tells me and his hands wander on the side of my hips. The warmth of his body at my back is such a comfort. Home. I close my eyes to enjoy it and lean into him.
Like a lightning bolt, a pair of ice-blue eyes jam into my head and I startle.
With a strange sense of guilt, I walk out of Luke's gentle touch, around the tank. The alien is pretty. Sparkly.
"How would such a creature ever die?" I ask.
"If you tore him apart to the point, where he cannot regrow his limbs, his brains, I suppose he would die."
I can see Luke's distorted face through the water. I know I'm a lucky woman to be with him.
"Could he just decide to not regrow?" I dig.
Luke chuckles. A warm sound. His voice is the perfect lower register.

"Why would he? He's better than all of us. Sees all, and has time on his side. He's a god."

I look at Socrates. A god. Somehow that is not what I pictured gods to look like.

"Wasn't it Socrates who said: "Death may be the greatest of all human blessings"?

That earns me another one of Luke's very sexy grins. He loves this. The vocal sparring. The clever back and forth. It's a turn-on for him.

"He also knew that he knew nothing."

He winks at me but then continues.

"This creature is the key. For humans. We'll have time not as a currency, but as a constant." His eyes are full of awe. If I didn't know better, I'd say he's in love with a jellyfish. And the way Socrates floats up and down for him and slow spirals, I'd figure that feeling was mutual.

"You would want to become like him? Live forever?" I ask, but I already know his answer.

"Who wouldn't? Death is just a disease for us to solve. You wouldn't have to decide anymore to just follow one passion. You could become everything you've ever wanted to be."

"Except not be."

He finally looks at me. Quizzically and taken aback.

He leaves his alien to his own devices and walks over to me, reaching for me with his hand. With some reluctance I don't fully understand myself, I let him pull me into a hug.

"I think you don't understand Socrates and he scares you. I'll keep you safe, babe."

He nips my ear but I wriggle out of the hold again. I need to be with my own thoughts. I walk back to the elevator without any explanation because I don't really have one.

"You're scratchy."

He's not wrong, but hearing it doesn't exactly help the matter. So with some annoyance, I offer: "I understand Socrates just fine. He's seen it all and understands the value of a definite end." Great, I'm projecting things onto a jellyfish.

63

The elevator door opens and I hesitate.

"Are you ok, love?" He asks, genuine worry in his voice. I turn to him, not even sure I know how to ask this.

"Did you have someone take the elevator up just before I came down? A new employee? A bit strange-looking?"

Luke raises an eyebrow and just points at a passing penguin.

"Those guys have been the only ones riding the elevator today. And as far as I know, we don't pay them. They really need to form a union."

I blink. Resigned. Unsure what to make of this strange day.

Up in the lobby, the morning light changes things. The first groups of people have populated the hallways and exhibits. With paper maps of the layout, discussions about priorities and the coolness of the various species fill every corner.

I stride through the clusters of excited visitors. At the door, I turn and stop by the security desk. I just have to know.

"Hey, George?"

His gentle face turns to me and brightens my own expression momentarily.

"Leaving us so soon? Were the penguins judgmental to you again?"

I laugh. They would make a great "Mean Girls" addition. "Can you do me a favor?"

His face turns a bit more serious.

"I had a strange encounter when I came in. Could you rewind the elevator camera and show me?"

Within seconds, he scans me up and down for injuries. "Did someone do something to you?"

I shake my head with so much vigor, that whiplash becomes a serious possibility.

"No, no, really. I just want to see and know that I'm not crazy."

He nods. Relief washing over his face. What a sweet human. He'd likely beat anyone to a pulp who would ever even think of hurting me.

64

The camera feed pops up. Shows me waiting in the elevator lobby. Hesitating. The door is closing. Almost. Then opening again. I step inside and my eyes trace after something that isn't there. Just as the door closes again.

He wasn't there. That strange figure was only in my head. I really am crazy. My heart races. That means, the girl falling from the roof, maybe her call, maybe the encounter on the subway, those ice-blue eyes. Was any of it real?

I stumble back and George catches me.

"Thank you. I must have just...I don't know. I'm sorry."

"Do you need a ride home? I can call someone."

I decline his kindness.

"Thank you. I'll be fine. Fresh air might be a good idea."

I smile and leave him behind, almost forgetting my bike, but he is so sweet to rush after me with it.

The air is frigid. The clouds hang low. For the moment it stopped raining.

Let's hope fresh air does the trick. Seeing things that aren't there isn't my idea of a good time. My heart races and pounds against the corners of my chest. I can only hope.

CHAPTER 13: THE NIGHT IT ALL CHANGED - LUKE

When the elevator goes back up three pairs of eyes follow it with utter confusion and worry. Mine and the two penguin chicks'. I look at the little fluffy fellows and hush them out of the way. They don't have any business down here to begin with. But they like my jellyfish as much as I do. Well, with different intentions, I guess. The little flightless birds look at my aliens like lunch in a fancy restaurant. And at me like a useless chef.

When Ness leaves, I sigh. Sometimes we have moments of friction. I try to not dwell on them. It's normal. What kind of couple would we be if we never fought, right? But lately, they are becoming more frequent. Since I bought the ring. The thought makes me smile. It sends a small pang of nervousness into the pit of my stomach too. I actually bought a ring.

I thought about it so long and with such care. I knew she wouldn't want a diamond. Not Ness.

She would want something with history, something old and different. Two weekends ago I went down to Savannah with my brother and visited every antique store in town. There's something haunted about that city. The rustling Spanish moss, the squares, and carriages. The old buildings and stories behind every stone.

And the ring I ended up finding. The store was an old, victorian villa. Not in pristine condition, but cared for. Three stories full of furniture, books, the smell of the revolution, and southern charm filled our day. It was fascinating. The owner told us tale after tale of his favorites and we ate it up. My brother is an art dealer, so this was like catnip for him. The owner brought out this old jewelry box, velvet of course, and opened it. Several rings in need of some professional cleaning. But I saw it right away. The deep, almost black ruby. The owner frowned.

"Probably not that one." He told me, which sparked my interest.

"It's pretty and all, but it was found in the Bonaventure Cemetery by the Freemason graves. Just popped up through the earth."

Just because of that, I was going to buy it. My brother's eyes widened too. This was it.

"You know about them Freemasons, right son?"

Yes, I did. The old oath-bound, secret society. I heard that a lot of the graves had the symbols on the tombstones here in the south. Deeply routed together with pirates and all the stuff making my nerd heart sing.

"I'll take it."

"But not as an engagement ring, surely? Look, here is a very lovely emerald." Too late.

My brother grinned from ear to ear. "Oh, she'll love this. Did you have it appraised?"

The store owner nodded, concerned and full of superstition.

"It's from 1765, older than this country. The ruby in the original setting. I'll sell it to you for -"

"I don't care, I take it." I blurted out, going against any bargaining technique ever invented.

We spent the afternoon getting drunk on the river. Oysters and beer and grinning like fiends. I bought a ring. When I came back, something changed. I looked at her with tenderness as though she was already my wife and could see it right away. Fear.

I don't know what she is so afraid of. We've been together for a while. We're family. I even asked her dad for permission. I knew he wasn't going to be around much longer and I just wanted to be able to give her that. That small piece of tradition. He was a lovely man. Kind and exceptionally wise. I wonder if Ness would be less afraid if he was still around.

So I sigh and go through my day wondering. The door flies open and Phil, the head trainer bursts in, anxious and out of breath.

"You ok?"

He is flustered and his cheeks are flushed. I've never seen the otherwise so organized man this way.

"Something is happening in the main tank."

"What?" I ask, but I'm already moving.

Sometimes I help him and the other trainers check on the sea creatures. They interact with them, but I'm a scientist. In theory, I know all the tricks.

Up in the pump room, a small crowd has already assembled. A few tour guides and two other trainers.

"Who's on the floor? Get back to work, we've got this." Phil chimes with faked confidence. Do we? Do we have this?

What is it that we have, I wonder and make my way through the big water pumps and filters.

This is the backside of the large aquarium tank. Not for visitors. I follow Phil up the slippery step ladder and step onto the grated platform. I've never been comfortable up here. It's always a little bit wobbly and feels unsafe. But that's not at all where my mind goes right now as I see the water below.

Red.

Blood red.

A feeding frenzy. Sharks dart around and attack the smaller and medium-sized fish. It's hard to make anything out.

"What happened?"

Phil is still in shock.

"I don't know. I think someone poured buckets of blood into the water to drive the sharks mad."

And that's exactly what they are. Mad.

They attack each other swimming through clouds of dark, red blood and clumps of what I can only hope to be fish-feed.

My jaw drops. This is not how feeding happens here. These sharks are over-fed on purpose at specific times to ensure a peaceful and child-appropriate experience for all visitors.

"We've got to close."

"We can't close, it's the weekend before the holidays, we have busses coming in." Phil is about to have a heart attack and I don't blame him.

I turn to him and squeeze his shoulder.
One of the larger sharks bursts through the surface. Almost a jump. The water splashes and partially covers us with salt and bits of red.
Phil is about to vomit.
"We've got to close." He nods. No energy for opposition.

We do close. To shut down an entire Aquarium on a busy day is quite the scenario. We all talk to frustrated guests and explain the "pump malfunction" in excruciating, fictional detail. No one wants to hear about a giant tank filled with blood, where their current favorite Nemo is dying.
Yes, I mean current. No one ever tells the kids this, but Nemos get replaced constantly. We even once had a break-in and all that was taken, were the clownfish. Don't get me wrong, I love the movie. But it started a wave that endangered an entire species.

A few of the dads are very upset and hard to console. Free passes are not a lot when there is a drive, babysitters, time in traffic, and other obstacles involved. I hear name-calling and the word unacceptable so many times, I shake my head and go back inside. It's my privilege as a scientist who just happens to be placed here. I don't have to deal with this.
I help out, of course, but I do have immortality to study. Maybe then I can make Nemo last longer. Priorities.

George joins me, still in his uniform, as I walk through the tunnel. The water is muddy and both of us frown at it. We walk to the main gallery. The one with the biggest window and the amphitheater seating. It's eerie when it's empty.
I can barely see anything through the water. Sometimes I just hear a splash and know it's not a moment of fun and fro-locking. George knows it too.
"We won't know the damage until the water clears." He states. Very matter-of-fact and very true. I nod.

"Do you think the big guys are gonna be ok?"
He means the whale sharks.
"Sharks don't usually attack them. They're too strong."
But I do wonder myself.
"The tank doesn't usually go bloody all the way either."
"No, it usually doesn't."
It means that after whoever threw buckets of blood in, many of our beloved creatures were attacked and a frenzy began, resulting in a lot more blood and death.
"Did you check the cameras yet?" I ask.
He sighs and nods.
"Checked them since Nessi left."
Only he calls her that and she hates it.
"Why?"
He turns in surprise.
"She didn't tell you? She saw someone strange in the elevator this morning when she came to visit you. But I never picked him on the feed."
My eyebrows bunch. That explains a lot though.
"You didn't pick him up anywhere?"
George shakes his head.
I get this very strange hollow feeling in my stomach. That one where you know something is off and about to become a lot more off, just when my phone rings.
"Hey?"
It's my future mother-in-law and she's worried.
"Have you seen her?"
"Yes, this morning." I look at my watch and somehow a lot of time has passed. It's nighttime.
"What's going on?"
I hear her hesitate.
"She went to work and then disappeared."
That wakes me up.
"What do you mean disappeared?"
She picks her words carefully. It tests my patience.
"Matt is here, her boss. He says she came, wasn't herself at all, and went outside for a cigarette - "
"Ness doesn't smoke." I intersect.

"I know, I know. But she went outside and didn't come back. I was hoping maybe she was with you?"

"I'll be right over."

I push the button and look at George.

"Can you lock up? I gotta go."

I don't see him nodding or protesting. I start into a run.

CHAPTER 14: GONE

It's so tense, that you could cut the air in the kitchen with a knife. Matt, Ness' bewildered boss, sits across from me and goes over the story again. The police officers follow his every word.

"She came in like she always did, a little off though."
"What was off about her?" One of the younger cops asks.
"She seemed anxious. Very anxious. One of her regular callers zoomed in and she passed it on to me and the new hire."
Matt's eyes widen. This means nothing to the officers so I clarify.
"Ness is very by the book, she would never pass on a client she cares about."
They nod and note it down.
"Then she asked me for a cigarette and said she needed fresh air."
There are a few more blank stares from the officers until Matt continues.
"She doesn't smoke. But I gave her a lighter and a cigarette and that's the last time I saw her."
My shoulders slump forward. There is a rational explanation for this, I know that. She's gonna come in laughing here any second. But there is dread building deep within me.
The officer sees it too.
"You're the boyfriend?"
I nod.
"He's more like a son-in-law." I smile but it's lopsided.
"Where were you this evening?"
I blink.
"What?"
"It's routine."
Suddenly I'm wide awake. This hits like a cold shower.
"I was in my lab. We had an emergency." I state.
"An emergency? With the fish?"

I could care less for the tone and his implications. But I stay calm.

"Yes, in fact. We had an emergency with the fish. Someone dumped buckets of blood into the shark tank and started a feeding frenzy. We closed the entire aquarium."

Matt's eyes grow even wider.

"Human blood?"

I hadn't even thought of that.

"I don't think so. I don't know."

There is a pause and I go over the possibility of this being a lot more sinister.

"So you haven't seen her since she left the aquarium this morning?"

"I haven't."

One of them walks over to the living room and starts calling someone. His colleague looks at me, explaining.

"He has to check your story. Rule things out."

I know they're just doing their job, but this still feels foul. On top of missing my girlfriend, and not knowing what's happened to her, I have to prove that I am in fact not connected to her disappearance.

CHAPTER 15: AN ADVENTURE - NESS

I'm still a little shaken when I arrive for work that night. I really should have called Luke and apologized for being, what did he call it? Scratchy.

I make a mental note of it. But I know that he's a very forgiving human being and probably just went straight back to work on his little aliens. It's such a different world in his lab.

I stash the bike, not even bothering with either of the wall mounts and head upstairs. Somehow, I'm burning up. Why is it so warm in the office?

I de-layer my onion-like appearance down to my thin, but very soft long sleeve. Matt already stares at me as though I've lost my mind. It's a strong possibility.

He heads my way and hugs me. That's very unexpected. He squeezes me and I pat his back. Why does he hug me? Is he dying? He's not really a hugging kinda guy.

He starts with: "I got a strange call today."

My heart sinks into the bottom of my feet.

"She's still alive?" I ask before I think.

His confusion is palpable. All over his face.

"What? Who? I got a call from the police asking how you were doing. You called 911 last night?"

I sigh. She didn't call in again. Of course, she didn't. It's daytime. Was she real at all? Did I make her up? I sigh in frustration.

A RING chimes through the quiet. Is that her?

"I'll get it." I declare loudly and jump across the office to press the button on the caller system.

Another RING.

It must be her. She's toying with me. Like a cat.

"Suicide Prevention Hotline, Ness speaking. Hello?"

The screen flickers to life and Emma comes into view. Her big eyes stare at me in surprise.

I can barely hide my disappointment.

"Hey, it's me." She says. Of course, it's her. I check my watch. Yep, her normal window. I step to the side. I can't do this right now. It wouldn't help anyone.

"Is something wrong?" She asks, worry clouding her face.

"You'll be speaking with Thomas today. I have to step out for a moment." I push the flustered new hire into the seat. Emma wipes her face. Distraught. Clinging to every word.

"But I really need to talk to YOU. I don't know Thomas." Thomas, the traitor, nods along with her and tells me: "I think it's much better if you took this - "

But I'm already walking. I can't breathe right. It feels like I'm not actually catching air.

In the hallway, Matt catches up with me. Now more worried than ever.

"That was really insensitive. What's going on with you?" Half of me just wants to tell him about all the weird pieces.

Instead, I ask: "Do you have a cigarette?"

"You don't smoke." I've never heard him sound so flat. Almost rude. He would make a great big brother. He fishes out his pack and a lighter and hands it to me.

"I need some air. I'll be right back."

I hurtle down the stairs and outside. One big, fresh breath of air. That feels so good. I don't even mind the rain soaking my thin shirt. I didn't bother with the sweater or the jacket or anything else. Just air. Air is good.

I step around the corner. The alley is darker but so close to the street, I would never think twice about it. From here you can hear the whispers of the crowds from the Fox Theatre.

I take another few deep breaths and start feeling myself again. Let's do this. I cinch the cigarette between my lips and roll the lighter wheel. I hate smoking. The smell, the action itself, only that first crackle of fire is nice. But I don't get that. I flip the thing again, but my hands and fingers have become stiff from the cold.

"Fuck" I exclaim out loud. I can't even be frustrated right?

But then I feel it. It's as reel as the frigid rain. Behind me. A cold huff of air. Like a long, soft exhale. The hairs on my neck stand up. Fear, genuine and undiluted pulses through my stomach. I know what this is. What have I been inviting into my life?

And then I hear footsteps. Wet shoes on pavement. Closer. Closer yet. Then they halt.

I gulp and realize how loud that sound can be. So very, very loud. With a lover's softness, Grace takes in my scent. Closer. From my shoulder up to her ear without touching her. But if I swayed just ever so slightly, my skin would feel her. I shiver. It's from the cold, I assure myself.

"Hello, Vanessa, Ness for short."

CHAPTER 16: NOT REAL

This can't be real. I step away from the words. Forward. Toward the street filled with real cars and lights and people. A deep inhale. All day, I wanted this to be part of my reality. Now, my stomach curls up inside me and I don't know what to do with this.

A flash from my dream passes by as I squeeze my eyes shut. Blonde hair, scraping teeth on the delicate skin of my wrist. I force my eyes open. This isn't helping the matter. So I do the only thing I can. I will face the empty alley behind me and once and for all make sure, that I have in fact, lost my remaining marbles.

I turn and face Grace. There she stands. Casually. With a small, lopsided grin on those beautiful, woven lips. Dark clothes, boots, and piercing, ice-blue eyes. She steps closer and lowers her hood. She is the most beautiful woman I've ever seen. But there is something inherently scary about her. The way she moves. Quiet, controlled. Like a jungle cat. Predatory. Stunning.

"Who are you?" I ask foolishly.

Grace cocks her head to the side and raises an eyebrow. Yeah, I do admit that's not my best moment, but it's so surreal. I'm still of half a mind to walk back up and pretend this isn't happening at all.

"Were you following me all day?"

She smirks and answers in sweet velvet softness. "I can't follow you all day."

Right. Of course. The day and night thing. I feel strange. Then she reaches out a hand. I stare at it as though I've never seen fingers before.

"C'mon, we don't have all night." She chimes. I'm confused and stare at her hand some more. Pristine. Like stolen from a Greek statue.

"What do you want?" I ask, surprising myself with the Xander.

"You didn't believe me yesterday." She states matter of fact.

"No, I don't think I did."

79

She smiles. Those lips move in sinful ways. "Then let me show you."

If it isn't real, I won't be able to touch it, right?

So I let my own shaking, insignificant hand connect with hers. This isn't real. This isn't real at all.

Her skin feels smooth. Cold, but so soft.

She guides me into the darkness of the alley. This isn't real. And if it were real, this would be a terrible idea. Why am I following this woman?

She lets go of my hand. With mesmerizing ease, she climbs upwards. I stand and watch her and see my own breath cloud dissipate in the freezing air.

I glance back at the street. Even with the rain and the cold, it seems to be the safer option. I sigh. This isn't real. It can't be. So I resign myself to exploring this strange un-reality and follow Grace up.

The rain still pelts down. It's slippery. I carefully try to keep my balance. I don't know how many flights we climbed. I wisely chose not to look down, because this isn't real. It's still part of this very odd day, that started with a very odd dream.

The view is great. Freeing in a way. We're above the hustle. The streets shine and glimmer. It's beautiful.

Grace is already at the edge. It makes me nervous. But every one of her steps has assuring security. Like an athlete in her element.

"Ready?" She asks me.

"Ready for wha-" but I don't even get to finish the sentence before she opens her arms wide and lets herself drop off the edge. I hear a THUD.

My heart skips a beat and when it restarts I think I'm still screaming. I cover my mouth.

Instinctively I fall to my knees and skit closer to the edge. I look down.

Nothing.

No body.

No mark on the street. Just darkness.

"Grace?" I whisper into the night. This cannot be real.

"I told you I cannot die."

I spin and there she is. Unhurt.

This little game is becoming problematic for my heart. It actually physically hurts now.

I blink at this strange, beautiful creature. She's indeed still alive. Not a hair out of place.

"This isn't real." I state for the first time voicing my thoughts.

She raises an eyebrow.

"I can jump again if you want me to."

I shake my head violently.

"No. What the fuck."

She smiles. It's maddening.

I scramble to my feet and approach her. Slipping on the roof tiles. Grace steadies me with one of those perfect hands.

"Careful. I'm pretty sure you would die."

She's a smartass. It's infuriating, but also extremely enticing. I should get away from her for a myriad of reasons. But I do no such thing.

Instead, I think about her hand touching mine. And I think she does the same. Her thumb graces across my skin. It sends a small shudder across my lower back.

I turn our grip over and examine her palm. Not a scratch. She let herself fall eight or nine stories and she's unscathed.

"Want to check my teeth next?" She jokes and smirks as I retract in horror. Yes, of course, I was too forward. Too curious. She's not a zoo animal. But at the same time, her smirk reveals beautiful and lethal canines.

I take my hand away.

"I'm sorry."

"It's alright." She assures me. I can't be the first human to have questions. This brings me to a very solid one. What happened to the ones before me?

But instead of voicing that, I ask. "What else can your body do that mine can't?"

She smirks and I blush. I feel stripped naked by her eyes. I did it again. The zoo animal curiosity. But she doesn't scold me. Instead, she takes a running leap. Without any

81

trouble, she lands on the neighboring roof. She's mesmerizing to watch.

With the graze of an old queen, she takes a mocking bow. "Mi'Lady"

I frown. Showoff.

Approaching the edge, I get a good view down. It's steep and much higher up than I thought. Fear creeps back in.

Grace jumps again. Wicked fast and far down. She lands on both of her feet, only to jump up again and touch down on the fire escape. Like a jungle cat. Lean muscle and skill.

With one arm she steadies herself against the building. The other bends the metal. A SCREACH. The metal GROANS. Another bend and the top level of the ladder now extends like a bridge between the roofs of the buildings.

I think my jaw dropped in awe a good while ago. No point in hiding it.

"Join me." She says. Playful and child-like. As though I would be jumping into a pond in the summer.

But I look at the ladder, precariously bridging the two buildings. Can I do this?

It isn't real, I tell myself and step forward. My foot is many flights above the ground on a makeshift bridge, covered in rain and ready to drop me to my death.

Another foot follows.

I'm so careful not to look down. I only have eyes for her over on the other side. A loud CLUNK takes me out of my confidence and rattles the ladder. Adrenaline shoots through me like a bolt. I fall to my knees, both hands clutching the ladder's sides. The drop is so deep. The rain falls calmly next to me. To each side. Steady. I try to look up but she's not there anymore. She's below me. Staring at me from beneath.

"Fear of heights?"

"Very much." I tell her.

"You have to face it."

She's right. I'm too far across to try to move backward. Careful, exploring, Grace touches my hands. Her fingers trace my own. It's sexy. Why would she do this now? There must be a safer moment to flirt. She has the gull to grin at me from underneath and wiggle her arching brows at me. I could strangle her. If I managed to move my hands from the ladder that is.

"You know what helps?" She asks.

Another touch. Featherlight.

"Distraction?"

"One limb in front of the other."

Grace slides her hand under the ladder forward. My hands follow atop. Interlacing fingers. Connected.

A bit wobbly, my legs follow. The fire-escape sways. I hold on tighter. Trying to will it to steady. Oh, I love control. I dare a look down. Darkness and wet street loom to greet me.

"Breathe. Ease your body."

I'm trying. "This doesn't feel safe." I tell her and I see her eyes crinkle with amusement.

"There is no such thing as safe."

Smartass. She's a smartass and she's not real. Another hand forward. This time I ignore the swaying of the damn ladder. Another hand. Another knee. Inches forward.

"You're not helping."

"Oh, so sorry." She chimes. "I'll catch you before you hit the ground."

Grace has reached the neighboring roof and pulled herself into a standing position. Casual. Her hand reaches out to me.

"I can't stand up."

I try. The ladder shakes dangerously.

"Why did you come with me?"

"You asked me to." I yell honestly.

She's making fun of me. "Do you always answer when death comes knocking at your door?"

"Apparently."

Another breath and my hand finds solid ground on the roof tiles. The other hand reaches for Grace, who pulls me up. Face to face. Close. Our breath clouds mesh and dissipate together into the cold night.

I touch Grace's hand again. Barely.

"How do you feel?" She asks, stroking her thump gently but without hesitation over the soft skin.

I surprise myself and smile widely. "Thrilled!"

Grace studies my face. For what, I do not know.

"You're welcome. So will you help me?"

Like a cold shower, it comes to me.

"Help you die?"

She nods and I take my hand out of hers.

"Why would you ever want to?"

She looks at me with a sincerity I can not stand.

"I need to die. When you kill, as I do, like I have to, you lose part of yourself every time."

I contemplate. There has to be a solution. Anything. But wouldn't she have thought of one already?

"Could You feed differently? Off of animals? Corpses?"

Her smile turns solemn. It breaks my heart. She shakes her head. A few raindrops run down her perfect face.

"It's not something I can fully control. Adrenaline, and fear, makes me turn into a hunter. I enjoy it in that moment. Love it."

I think if I could move like her, I would too. The speed. The ease. I look her straight into her ice-blue eyes and ask the essential question.

"What if I don't? You're gonna kill me?"

She blinks. Matter of fact.

"No one has known me long and lived to tell the story."

I touch Grace's lips. Soft. Slightly parted. I don't know how I've suddenly become so brazen but I just had to. She doesn't shy away from me. But there is surprise on Grace's face. It's intimate.

"You would kill me?"

A breath heats my finger as Grace opens her mouth wider. There. Razor-sharp. Teeth. I let my finger slide over one. Grace gently removes my hand.

"Even if I wouldn't want to, that side of me can take over."

Her teeth are beautiful.

"I need to see what it's like." I tell her.

There's a long moment between us. Eye to eye. I'm not sure whether she's about to put those pillowy lips on my mouth to kiss me, or on my throat to rip it clean out. Then Grace pulls away. She heads towards the ladder down and gestures for me to follow her. So without a thought, I follow.

CHAPTER 17: ALLURE - GRACE

How to lure a human.
Step one - be confident. Bordering on arrogance. I've found that to be strangely successful. Yes, I know, it's odd to me too. But walking in like you own the place seems to really do the trick. In my few centuries of existence, I found it to be very effective.
I once told a stock trader in the late 1920s which bets to place with such conviction, he put his life's savings down. For me it was just a little exercise in seeing whether I can be convincing. I can. His hungry eyes, full of greed and hope still sometimes come back to me in a dream. So much excitement to strike it big. All the money in the world couldn't have saved him from me though. I was hungry too.

Step two is mystery. Humans love the unknown. It gives them hope. There is no true logic to it, but I think it affirms their believes in positive possibilities. If something like me exists, there have to be angels too, right? So I tend to play with that idea. At least I leave it open-ended for them. It's really a kindness.
I have never once met an angel and I've been around a long time. And before you ask, no, I haven't met ghosts or werwolves or any of the other messy creatures of novelists imaginations either. Frankly, I'd love to meet a werewolf. Can you imagine? You live a normal live and then once a month you turn into a vicious animal for a night and get to live out all your anger.

That sounds better to me than my existence. I have lived in this state of hunger since that night. Since that crazy night my father saved my life. I think now is as good a time as any to tell you about that night. It was back in 1675. Before this city was officially a city and right around the time when people started burning women who dared to ask questions. Joyful period. Truly.

Before I was even born, my father had immigrated and met my beautiful mom in what is now Macon, Georgia. She was a southern girl through and through. Properly raised, from new money and she had just had her coming out ball on her parents estate.

But she met my father one evening by the river, playing his violin and entertaining the pondering minds. She couldn't keep her eyes off him.
A spark in his eyes and this charming, slightly rough accent. He played and fiddled until her heart was his.
Of course her parents didn't want her to marry a newly immigrated, penny-less man without any connections. My lovely father asked for my mother's hand and received conditions instead of permission. Make money and be respected.
Now, they didn't know my dad. He was a very smart and crafty man. Once he wanted something, he would move heaven and earth to get it. So he studied the layout of the local settlements outside of the big plantations. For the rest of the summer, he plaid his violin at every outing, every get-together and in between. With the money from that and a loan from a wealthy spice trader, he managed to buy land deep in the Oconee Forest. Between peach trees, banana spider nets and mossy rustle, my dad built a grain mill.
He was a doctor, and a great one at that. But he needed the locals to trust him first. People didn't really believe in science and rather agreed to blood letting and injecting poisonous silver, than actual medicine. Somehow my father managed to do both. He hired a few helping hands for the mill to operate and within six months, he managed to make enough to pay back half the loan and buy my mother a ring. To the dismay of her dad, she married him.

I can still see his smile when he looked at her. I remember that as a small child. They just stopped in normal moments and looked at each other. Then one of them would grin. That lovely, true grin that you cannot help.

They still felt that way. Both of them. All the way up until that night.

That night I will never be able to forget was 1692. My that time my dad was established and well respected. The mill had its own road, albeit it just being pressed dirt, but it connected to the city and a small school we had founded a few years prior. I actually taught the smaller children there. I was fourteen so I just went over the basics with the little ones. Reading and writing. For all of them. I loved it. My father had taught us early and always wanted us to be able to make up our own minds. I realized only much later how special that was for that time.

But some of the children's parents didn't agree. Especially for girls. I remember how appalled some of the upper glass mothers were that a woman, a girl, was teaching. I should be preparing to come out to society and find a husband, not fill their children's heads with nonsense. That's how it started.

At home my father went much further than that of course. He was a doctor. So when I showed interest in medicine, he taught me. Everything. Early.

I could tell you the difference between the patella and the Achilles tendon by the age of four. I once scared my mother by telling her I had a hematoma. You see, dad had taught me all the Latin and Greek words, so instead of telling her I'd fallen and bruised my knee, I wobbled around sounding odd. I may have been an odd child. Especially for that time. But I loved my father and all of his lessons.

The first time he let me observe an autopsy was the only time I saw my parents argue. My mother thought I was too young at thirteen. But I ended up convincing her by telling her how much good I could do if I become a doctor, who, like my father, believes in science. How much knowledge I might be able to add over time.

So she let me watch. Any normal child, or person, would have been shocked at the brutality and gore. But my father had taught me how to separate and compartmentalize. A body is just that. A body. A biological machine. Any dead one broke down and it's our job to figure out why. I watched as the first scalpel went into the skin and it parted like a smooth zipper. There was something beautiful about that simplicity. He showed me the different scalpels and how to use them. Which cut is good for what and why. I still use that knowledge, but in a very different way. Back then, I used scalpels to understand the build of homo sapiens sapiens. See? This is what happens when your father overdoes it with the Latin lessons.

He taught me what to look for within that human machine. What people died from and why. It was fascinating. I wish he had also taught me what people believed they died from. And why this believe system was so deeply routed in fear, opposing science at every turn. Progress at every corner. That would have avoided my fateful outcome.

The night in question started fairly normal. We had just picked up a new corpse from the local cemetery. My father always paid the undertaker handsomely to keep him quiet. But today he had been a bit strange. He didn't look us in the eye. I wish that had been another one of my father's lessons. Human behavior.

At the mill, I waited patiently down in the study below the shoot for dad to slide the body through. We had a very good system. The study was more of an old timey morgue. We had two gurneys, tools, a cooling unit filled with ice every day and my father's scalpel box. Big jars with specimen of different kinds filled the shelves. A human heart, a few eyeballs. Most people would run screaming. My younger sister always did. As always, I knew she was hiding somewhere and watched us take the body in. Sarah was eight and equally scared and fascinated. I heard her rustling out in the hallway. She was never very good at hiding. The thought still makes me smile.

90

I remember peering up the metal shoot and seeing the wrapped corpse already half way inside.

"May I let go?"

Dad was always so polite.

Before I could answer, the thing CLATTERED down loudly and landed on the gurney, spewing dust everywhere. I remember looking at the body with him. Another one that had passed off consumption. It's become quite the epidemic.

My dad was ahead of his time. He truly was. Everyone else believed this body to be something entirely different. The nails were still growing. The skin was pale, the lips blood red and speckles of dried blood were in the corners of the mouth.

Worse, when we had pulled back the sheet, the villagers showed us exactly what they thought this man was. They had staked him to his own coffin. Through the heart. A large hole where the heart should be.

And then the corpse sat up. Suddenly with no warning.

I remember hearing my little sister scream in utter panic and running up the stairs. She was an adorable, little girl.

The next thing I remember is smoke. My father looked at me with this all knowing face. Something in him knew. He whispered an apology. Then he yelled at me to try and safe my sister. The villagers had come to burn down the mill. Science and progress. We were an abomination. That weasel of an undertake had ratted us out.

I remember running upstairs and hearing my mother scream. I still smell the smoke and the ash. Hear the shouts.

"Devil's spawn."

"You aim to raise the dead."

"Witchcraft."

I remember wanting to tell them and show them the simple explanation. But my father had taught me well. One cannot argue with fear.

So I tried and failed to save my sister. Up in her room they found us. She was hiding and I told her a poem.

91

Last night upon the stair
I saw a man who wasn't there.
He wasn't there again today
Oh, how I wish he'd go away.
But he didn't go away. Five of them came in. One grabbed me and slit my throat from ear to ear and make me watch as they dragged my sister out from under the bed. They called her a demon child and broke her neck. I watched as her little life ebbed and halted. So quickly, I barely registered the details. I was bleeding and fading. I only remember bits and pieces from the rest of that night. I remember my father entering and screams starting. I still see one of the men pleading for his life. But I don't know what my father did. Brave doctor, scientist and wonderful husband to my mother who was lying dead in the next room.
When he was done killing, he picked me up. Wheezing. I was wheezing through the blood. Fading.

"Last night upon the stair."

He carried me into the morgue as the mill burned. But the morgue was cold and dark. He apologized. I remember him apologizing and telling me that he wished he could save me from this fate. That he didn't want this for me. He wished he could tell me the rules.

What rules? I remember thinking.
"I saw a man who wasn't there."

He kept telling me to drink something. It was warm. Warm and faintly smelling of iron.
As the light faded with me, my drank. And drank.
"He wasn't there again today"

Hunger overcame me. I drank.
"Oh, how I wish he'd go away."
Then we both burned to cinders.

CHAPTER 18: NEW ME

Step three in luring a human.

Thrill. I've found danger to be the most intoxicating and effective poison you can offer to humans. Dancing with death makes them feel alive. There's a sexual component to it too. That idea of being invincible. They don't understand that it's not they who are invincible at all. But they get to taste it.

When I woke up after the fire, naked in the ashes, the villagers had left. It was evening again and the crickets were yelling their nightly song of southern charm. I remember being confused, heartbroken, scared and very, very hungry. I searched through the rubble of the mill but my family was dead. I found my mother's necklace and my sister's shoe. Only one. That's how hot the fire had burnt.
There was no remanence of my father. Anywhere. The good doctor Tepeš Lucârd was wiped off the face of the earth.

Deep in the old morgue, I found his metal cupboard with scalpels. All of them. Not a thread of clothing and no empathy left, I went to wipe out a village. I didn't know then what was happening to me, or how strong I was or anything like that. I didn't care if I died again. So I strapped as many of my father's scalpels to my body as I could and went hunting.
The first stop was easy. The cemetery was close and quiet. The little adjacent chapel stood stark against the midnight sky. So pretty.

I looked through the window and saw the old undertaker occupied by his favorite past-time. Drinking. By his movement I could guess he was about half a bottle of moonshine in. He stank. Somehow I never noticed how much he reeked. I waited until he went outside to relieve himself by pissing on a freshly dug grave. Heathen. This is the kind of God-fearing man who called my family the spawns of the devil?

"Good evening." My voice sounded the same. I found that so surprising. He stumbled around. I will never forget that dumbfounded expression on his face. All he must have seen was this 19-year-old woman he killed yesterday. Not the rage. Not the utter emptiness inside.
It was almost instinctual. Smooth. I knew exactly where to cut. He didn't even raise a hand. Too drunk and in disbelief. I sliced from the groin up to his ribs and made sure my hooked knife hitched a little bit. No mercy for the rat.
The scent of his blood hit me at once. For the first time I felt a change in my eyes and felt stronger. Before I knew what I was doing, I drank him dry.
He tasted vile. Sick. Faintly rotten. I tried to throw it up but my own body didn't comply. After a few moments it settled. I took his clothes and vowed to replace them as soon as possible, as I made my way into the village.
I started with the mayor's house. He allowed this to happen and he was my father's friend. He saw me coming. When I marched towards his front door through his gate, he held up a crucifix. He prayed. Just like my mother did last night. Except my mother did it for the wellbeing of my sister and me. This little, fat man did it to save his own hide.
With him, I had the sudden urge to play like a cat does with her second mouse. Not too hungry, enough time to have a little fun.
So I pulled a small scalpel and watched it fly through the air. You see, dear reader, scalpels are not like knives. The weight is different. I wanted to test just how they work if I throw them. Let me tell you, they do fairly well. My first shot nicked his carotid.
The second just made his crucifix land on the steps of his grand entry way. I picked it up and to show him how little I cared about anything after last night, I hung it around

my own neck. Its weight sat cold against my sternum. I remember his eyes widening and his chubby, little hands scrambling for anything to throw at me.
But I grabbed him by the throat.
"I was right. We were right. You are the devil's spawn."
I let him finish his little process and squeezed my hand. So fragile. Skin and bones. So very fragile. My hand went straight through his flesh without much effort at all. Another gulp and no more words emerged from his hateful heart. I licked my bloody hands clean and went on my merry way.

From house to house. Sometimes I let them speak, sometimes I killed them quickly. But by the end of the night, I was wearing a beautiful, silk dress, leather shoes and had even found better leather straps to tie my scalpels to me. They would become my jewelry over the years.
I didn't feel anything. Not for a long time. I don't know what exactly I became that night, but the death toll was attributed to an outbreak of consumption. Of course.
The neighboring priest and his flock buried all the bodies staked to their individual coffins. For a month I watched them pray every night that no revenants may rise from the graves.

Well, nothing rose from the graves. It was already amongst them. Helping them bury and pray and nod at the strange tales of the mill fire and the village struck down within one, single night.

CHAPTER 19: THE BOOKS WERE WRONG

I went through a dark period. Killing for sport. Decades passed and I barely felt anything. Here and there I met a handsome soldier and caught the flutters of my former heartbeat. But it always ended badly. For the ones I met.

Then a century ago, the romantics came along and with them the dark tales of vampires. I devoured those books. Each and every one of them. I loved Bram Stoker. Part of me hoped he knew someone like me. That his tales were based on truth. I tried biting and giving blood, creating an equal. A companion. I had been the only one of my kind. I was so hopeful. But all of my efforts resulted in more disappointment and resentment of the world. Stoker was wrong. I can eat garlic. The sun doesn't kill me. It makes me disappear, but I reappear when the night creeps back. A stake through the heart, a silver bullet, removing the head and burning...

I have tried it all. The gruesome lord with his fetish for virgins was clearly not a family relation. I'm still the only one like me I've ever met. Except. I think my father was like me. But I don't know. I wish he had told me. He was so wise and kind. It would have been a kindness to either let me die that night with the rest of them, or to teach me what I am. He did something. And as much as I try to remember, all I see is smoke and darkness. His voice. Fire.

Those images stand in stark contrast to the winter chill of the city. It's cold enough that I can see Ness' breath forming a little cloud in front of her face. Luring her required no effort at all. I simply asked. She willingly followed. My nightingale. My beautiful, innocent, lost nightingale. I lead us through the city. My shortcuts surprise her. We walk through the old train-yards. Atlanta built on top of already abandoned tracks and roads. So for someone like me, it's the perfect playground.

We've walked in silence. Her delicate hand has reached out to my own with that careful question a few times. I dare not to answer. She wanted to see what I am and how I live. If I should truly die. So I took her here. The moment she sees, her hand won't be reaching out. Neither will her heart.

For her sake, I hope that she doesn't panic. Fear in humans triggers the hunter in me. It's instinctual and it's sudden and something I cannot control. I have half a mind of telling her. Don't be afraid. What ever you do, don't be afraid. Don't run. If you run, you're dead. But it's like telling someone to not think if a pink elephant in the room. All they will be able to think about is...a large, pink elephant.

So silent walking it is.

The darkness shrouds us bit by bit. The old tracks lead deep into the underground halls. Long forgotten. No train has left this place in decades. They rumble above. Ness looks up at the noise and I can see her heartbeat pump blood through her pretty neck. Don't be afraid.

I move further. The old train cars stand dilapidated and forlorn. Graffiti and piss adorn them all with equal artistry. Here we go.

The rust brown one is my current home. Long ago, when I started killing, I lived in the places of my...food. Picked the rich and powerful. But I kept having to run and being chased and burned. This way, people leave me alone and I can hide in the shadows as I wish.

I step onto the doorway. Ness hesitates. Smart. She should turn around now and go home. She should pretend I'm not real and made up entirely.

"What is this?" She asks?

Oh I can hear the hesitation in her voice. It's not fear. But it's not confidence either.

I hand her the flashlight I stashed in the corner.

"So you can see better." I tell her.

"It smells funny."

I nod. Pausing.

"You don't have to go in if you don't want to. You can turn around and go home."

She looks at me straight. Open. It breaks my heart. My nightingale trusts me implicitly. If I told her to jump, she would jump. The one thing she wouldn't do, however, if turn around to safety and whatever life she knew.

She clicks on the flashlight. Dim and solemn the little light fights against the darkness of Pullman's yard and its abandonment. I can see the dust particles dancing.

She steps inside.

I smell her inherent shock first. That rush of adrenaline through her heart into every part of her body. The scent is electrifying. Not in a good way. For her.

Ness stumbles backwards. Into me.

I knew she couldn't handle this.

My latest catch, so to say, is hung up by his feet. Arms slack to his sides. The old, sick man is shirtless and I put a bucket under his head before I split his neck wide open to let him bleed out. He's been here for a few days after I collected him on the subway and made sure he'd die soon regardless of my sudden...introduction into his life.

His name was John. He was 75 years old and had been a factory worker once. A long time ago. We talked for a long time while I bought him his favorite poison, whisky and he told me how he ended up on the streets. His family hadn't spoken to him for many years and alcohol had long been his closest companion.

I could smell death on him even before he ever told me he was addicted to the bottle. A fatty liver shows and smells. So I asked him if he wanted to stick around. I remember him smiling broadly and shaking his head. I made it quick for him of course. Took him here. Laughed with him. Reminisced a bit about the wonderful years when he felt good. And then I killed him without him suspecting any danger. He never felt any pain.

But Ness sees his body swaying. Dirty, dark and very dead. His milky eyes stare at her and she is hit with the full scent of decomposition. If you don't know that tell-tale mix, it smells sickly sweet. Like a southern candy story by the river turned bad in the sun. Vile.

She stumbles back into me and I let her out of the train car. But her adrenaline is rising quickly. Dangerous. I hold myself back but I can feel it coming over me. The hunt. It's automatic. My eyes zone in and out of it. They shine silver when I kill.

I turn to watch my nightingale hyperventilate. Fear. That is fear on her. My eyes zone in on her and the world blurs.

CHAPTER 20: THE THING ABOUT FEAR

Ness doubles over and I watch her trying to inhale air. But my vision is focused in on her in the wrong way.
I grip the rusted door frame.
"Breathe." I rasp lowly. All I can do.
I don't feel my strength anymore. IN this state of mind, I never do. The door frame crumbles into my fingers. Speckles of rusted metal flake to the ground like fiery snow. My feet follow her out. I see only her.
"You're going to have to calm your breathing or the adrenaline in your blood makes you smell like...prey."
She takes in another gulp of air. Yapping. I smell it filling her lungs. Smell her blood in her veins. I squeeze my eyes shut as hard as I can.
"I can smell -"
She interrupts me. Brave human. Facing me. Still heaving.
"Currently all you're gonna smell... Is my asthma acting up."
My blur refocuses.
She manages an inhale. Good.
My vision comes back.
Another step back. Another breath. Slowly.
My hand lets go off the crunched lock I ripped right out of the door. It clinks to the ground.
Ness looks at me. Not afraid. Just herself.
"You really kill people."
Not a question. I nod. Giving her nothing but truth.
"It's not a choice. I've gone days without it. Then it overcomes me and I kill without a thought."
I point at the train car.
"If I manage it, schedule it, I can pick someone sick or old."
She nods. "Someone you think 'deserves to die'."
"No. Just someone much closer to death to begin with."
Her asthma really must have gotten the best of her. She falters and sits down on the cold, hard floor.

At least she doesn't run. That would have sealed her fate. I wouldn't have had the time or the strength to control my instincts. She would have been dead within seconds.

I sit next to her. Giving her space enough to recoil if she needs to. But she doesn't. She's still trying to calm herself.

"When I was little my father used to tell me this poem to help me calm down. It's a scary old ghost story, so it never worked. But it stuck."

She doesn't turn to look at me, but inclines her head for me to continue.

"Last night upon the stair -"

"Oh, I think I know that one." She interrupts me with her hand on my arm. I feel her warm skin bleed its heat through my thin layer of clothing. Alive.

"I saw a girl who wasn't there.

She wasn't there again today.

Oh, how I wish she'd go away."

I can't help the smile that blooms on my own face. She knows my little poem. Odd and wonderful. And she changed it too. In her version its a girl.

"Do you know the second verse?" I ask her.

Her head spins to me. All fear forgotten. Replaced by curiosity.

"Second verse?"

"She loves a songbird, pure and fare.

A nightingale, a song of air.

Of innocence, of life and yearning.

A bird of love, but dead, come morning."

Her heart beat slows as the words sink in. A low chuckle.

"You made that part up."

I don't have to answer. It is again not a question. My nightingale knows me quite well.

She studies my face and her delicate fingers play with the fabric of my sleeve.

"You're going to kill me."

Ah, that. I take her hand and interlace our fingers as I lay down flat next to her. Staring at the ceiling of this forgotten, urban cave.

"Not if you kill me first. You'd be doing the world a favor."

I don't see the tear sprouting and running down her soft cheek, but I smell the salt. Her head bumps into mine. A comfort. A solace.

"How?" She asks.

CHAPTER 21: HOW TO DIE TWICE - NESS

This night might be the strangest adventure of my life. Yet, I'm still here. I haven't turned back to the office after this peculiar woman appeared in an alley to seduce me to follow her up a ladder. I didn't call the police when she let herself fall off the roof. Completely against my training.

I sat there and gaped when she reappeared. Full of wonder. She didn't die. She didn't have a single scratch on her beautiful, sleek form.

I didn't question following her across rooftops, full well knowing I'd risk my own hide. Something about Grace blinds me with awe. The fascination led me here. Into the old Pullman Yard. A place I was taught to avoid after dusk. Really during any time, but especially when the night fell. Drug-dealers and the shadows of society were supposedly taking hold of this territory. Nothing good happened here if I recall the tales.

While they were right, I don't think they fully accounted for what I just witnessed. It still sits in my bones. The image of the body swaying. Hung by the feet. Dripping blood and slowing filling a bucket below.

Drip.

I shudder as I hoist myself up onto another roof. Grace told me her story. She told me what happened when she woke up in this new body. Her months of vengeance. I listened intently. Lying on the concrete floor of this forgotten place, playing with strands of her hair. I should have run.

She told me how after a few years she'd been found out once. Discovered for what she was. She had married. I felt a small pang of unwarranted jealousy. Deep in my stomach. Grace had fallen in love and married a wonderful, kind man. But he found his new bride very strange. To only entertain at night. Not to want to have tea or luncheons. She pretended to be very sensitive to the sun. An illness. At first he understood. But his mother got wary and finally he got angry with her and one day yanked the curtains open. The pain was indescribable. She couldn't help myself. Couldn't control it. Her adoring, young love died in a frenzy of her rage and when she came back to normal, she could barely remember what she had done.

In that moment I understood why she wanted to die. She wouldn't be able to love someone openly without fear of killing them. Ever. I graced her porcelain skin under the lobe of her ear. Where the sensitive part of her neck made her hair rise to my fingers' command.

She continued telling me the story. How she inherited the house. But her mother in law didn't let up. One day, when Grace was locked away in the darkness, her husband's mother brought the town registrar and the mayor with her. They burned her at the stake that night. No trial. No questions. That pain was worse than death.

I gulped. I never thought I would agree to help someone die. Let alone become part of this elaborate, crazy plan we're now enacting. But in that moment. I nodded and I agreed. Not because she would likely kill me otherwise. Somehow I am not afraid of her.

Now we stand on the old, rusted beams on the roof. The train cars rest below. And I'm holding a gun.

I've never held one before. The cold metal cools my palm.

My hands are shaking and my heart skips a beat. This is crazy. I'm holding a gun, pointing it at a person. No, I remind myself. Not a person. Someone who seized to be a person long ago.

"Safety is off. All you have to do is -"

Grace is trying to calm me down, but it's not working one bit.

"This is insane. I can't do this."

This isn't real, I tell myself. But this stupid gun feels about as reel as the wobbly roof sheets below.

"Why can't you shoot yourself?" A question I never thought would come out of my mouth.

"I've tried. I think it might have to be someone else doing the deed. A human." I blink at her. It doesn't make sense.

106

Not fully. But nothing about this crazy night made sense to me and yet...

I exhale and hold the revolver. My hands are shaking. So is the damn gun.

Grace comes closer and tells me to hold it with both hands and breathe. Somehow that irks me. Similar to telling someone in an argument to calm down. I start pacing and waving the silly weapon through the air.

"I can't shoot you. I can't shoot anyone." It's true. I save lives. It's my job. I talk people out of this sort of scenario.

"Yes you can." She's steady. Ready to die.

It makes me even more nervous.

"You picked the wrong person. I try to save people." I'm shouting. I don't know why, but it's a small release of the confusing emotions bubbling up inside of me.

"You would be saving me." I can't argue. She's right.

"Why me?"

She smiles. Such a sad smile. So beautiful.

"You picked up the phone."

I take a deep breath. Vampires are not real. This is not real. Grace approaches. She places the gun against her chest. Her hand on mine. Strokes my cheek. Soft and calming. Our eyes meet.

"Just pull the trigger."

"No."

"Come on. Just one little flick of your finger."

I shake my head. No. I can't shoot her.

She cups my head softly with one hand. Strong but not forceful. Brow to brow we stand and I stare into her ice blue eyes. Mesmerizing. Like the ocean in a tropical land. I lose myself in them. A huff of a breath escapes me and gives away my utter helplessness. I lower my eyes. My head clears when I see the partial roof and the concrete looming far, far below.

"Look at me." Grace says and caresses my ear with her thumb. This is not fair.

"No." I can resist her. She isn't real.

But Grace doesn't play fair. Swift and smooth, she snags my jaw and presses a kiss onto my lips. The world seizes to spin. Her lips are soft and cool. A small noise escapes my throat.

Defenses down. Grace retracts, smiles at my surprised face, and forces my finger to PULL THE TRIGGER.

A SCREAM escapes me as the SHOT RINGS clear.

Grace falls back and plummets through the broken beams down. DOWN.

For a moment, the night goes silent. I hear no cars in the distance, no sirens, no rain, not a single noise of the usual cacophony that shrouds the city in busy life. The shot reverberates in the air and in my bones.

Then I blink and snap back to reality.

I drop onto my knees. Scanning the floor below. I see the train car. The spot where we laid and shared stories.

There. Wood and pieces of plaster, but Grace stares up at me, lifeless. She's dead.

CHAPTER 22: DAWN

It takes me way too long to climb down from the roof. I break the skin on my wrists and scratch my jeans. I don't care. The pain feels kind of good. The rush of adrenaline makes my head pound. I keep turning my head and I see Grace.
Lying still between the beam she took down with her during the fall and the grey, half broken glass window. Light creeps in. Brighter. The morning isn't too far off. I jump the last few steps and my knees burn in response. Too high for my untrained body. My bones click in protest. But I ignore them. They don't get a say in this. I hurl to the lifeless form and examine her. Her serene but cold face. My hands rove over her skin. Her eyes shine brightly upward. Ice-Blue but no life within them.
I check her neck. I take her by the shoulders and shake her. Her hair falls in waves and catches the light. I shake her harder. Frantic and in disbelief. She told me that she cannot die. She used me. A flurry of emotion overcomes me and shakes my insides. Nothing seems broken. She looks serene. The old rusted metal beam acquired much more visible damage than Grace. And yet...
Not a breath breaks her beautiful lips.
My own breath threatens to stutter in my chest as I look at her and realize -
I SCREAM and cover my mouth as I stumble back in shock and wonder.
Grace sits up with one strong and precious intake of air. Bright eyes flaring silver for just a moment. She stares at me. A small smile on her lips.
"You're alive." I rasp and hear my voice. I've been crying ugly tears and didn't even realize it.
"Whatever that means." She says and shakes the ache out of her long limbs. One by one.
I approach and take her hand. "Let's never do that again." I beg.

"We won't have to. It clearly wasn't working." She tells me but I'm not in the mood to even chuckle. Relief washes over me and I start to feel warm again.

I take her face between my palms and lean my forehead against hers. My warmth creeps into her. Some life.

Her eyes flicker to the window. The first rays of daylight creep through the clouds. For once, it's not raining.

"Distracting me like that isn't fair." I tell her. She knows what I mean.

"You didn't want me to kiss you?" She asks almost sheepishly. But her eyes betray the mock innocence behind the question. There is hunger in them. It sends a pang of a different kind into the depths of my stomach. My core feels molten.

Grace shifts and hisses in pain. She tries to hide it, but too late. My eyes dart over every inch of her. her hand. The light. THE LIGHT. Her hand starts fluttering like dust particles. It almost glitters when it catches the rays of sunshine. I've never wanted it to be cloudy again more than I do right now. She's disappearing before my eyes.

"No, no." I hear myself stuttering.

She smiles grimly.

"You might only have one chance to try to kiss me again."

I take her shoulders and try to move her. But the light is quicker. Inch by inch, Grace turns into dust like small fireflies on a starry night. The frantic fear inside of me returns with a vengeance. What can I do? There must be something I can do?

"Look at me." Grace orders.

"Stay." I order her right back.

Her arm hazes into ash and a light breeze carries it away like dark snowflakes. Beautiful.

"Look at me." She repeats and her voice strains.

Grace's entire body seams to transition. Brow to brow. I hold her face in my hands.

I stroke her hair. Then she kisses me. Lips on lips. Hesitant. Exploring. An offer and a question. Soft but not shy.

110

I close my eyes, freezing in place. Still unsure. Feeling those full, sinful lips, wanting more.
Finally, Grace's head too, fades into dust.
Gone! A lonely ray of sunlight pierces through the broken roof. A spotlight to the empty spot, where Grace just laid broken.
In fury and pain, I turn to it and SCREAM at the sunshine.

CHAPTER 23: WHO ARE YOU? - LUKE

It's been a very long night. The police officers have continued to check in with us every few hours. One remained stationed here to make sure he'd be here for Ness' return.

Part of me thinks, however, he stayed because of me. They didn't trust me. I'm Ness' boyfriend and I must have something to do with her disappearance. I can't even be mad at them. If I came to a house and someone was missing, I'd suspect the partner too.

I've been sitting here, nurturing my whiskey for the better part of an hour without a word. Just watching my wonderful mother-in-law, Beth, and the officer. I think he's desperately trying to flirt with her. This guy has terrible timing.

"So how long have you lived here?" He asks her, but his hands shift nervously from his pockets to his hips as he tries to lean against the door frame and, to my amusement, misses. He stumbles a bit but catches himself.

Beth indulges him. She's such a sweet woman.

"It feels like forever. I've always liked Victorian architecture." She smiles a bit. That practiced, polite expression that looks almost painful.

The officer nods and returns his hands back to the pockets for no reason.

"Oh, so you like architecture? There are a lot of interesting spots all over Atlanta nowadays. They really changed the city quite a bit." He's fishing and has very little idea. But Beth smiles again. Part of me is even grateful for his distraction. She needs it. So do I.

"I love the historical preservation of the buildings. Did you know that the local art school has an incredible historical preservation program?"

He fakes even more interest and pulls a chair, eyebrows drawn together in false fascination. I almost roll my eyes.

Is this what flirting looks like when you get older? Or does he just not have good game?

I squint. Through the kitchen window a rare sight during this time of year, sun-flares. It's already morning. This long, arduous and hard night is finally bleeding into dawn. The sun peaks through the cloud cover. Probably won't stay, but it takes me out of my trance. I take a deep breath and another sip of the Glenlivet Beth poured to calm us down. It helped for a moment. For a short hour or so. When we told the officers everything we could possibly think of about Ness. Matt told them about her work and dedication to rules and clients. He choked up when he told them why she was so relentless about suicide. That's when Beth emptied her own glass in one smooth drop. She didn't want to think of her late husband. But there is no denying that it affected Ness deeply. Matt went over and over and over the events of this night. She arrived at work. Disheveled and not herself. She denied a call with one of her regular callers. Something she would never do. And then, she asked for a cigarette and fresh air, went outside, and hasn't been seen again. I found myself clinging to every detail. Analyzing. Thinking with them and trying to see what happened. I know that part of the city like the back of my hand. The alley and the restaurant next door are on the bottom floor of the tall building. I close my eyes and picture it again. The lights from the fox theatre creeping across the street.

Matt is now thoroughly passed out on the couch in the living room across the hall. One drink and it took him out. I'm still thinking. And clearly being analyzed.

I went over my story too. So many times. Filled in times as best as I remember, every small detail and every location. They should now know more about my research than my assistant. Maybe they'll solve immortality. But then I look at officer hot stuff over there trying his best to have a conversation about historical preservation in architecture. He nods a lot. So much nodding. And even though he sat down, his hands still rove back from his pockets to the seat and to his knees. He has no idea what to do with them.

Something catches my eye and I turn to look out of the kitchen window. The sun is covered again by the grey clouds and mist of the morning. I resign to the gloom and empty my glass. Might as well. Then I hear steps.

I rise and pat to the front door. Beth and the officer are still deep in conversation. I've been getting up and randomly checking the door a lot this night. So they don't bother to follow me.

I hear it clear as day. Keys. I yank the door open and my heart nearly stops. There she is. Ness. Disheveled and her face an expression I have never seen before. She is holding a gun. It dangles closely from her hand. Before I can think, my eyes widen at it and it pulls Ness into reality. She pockets it. Hiding it from sight.

I pick her up into a hug. A high-pitched yelp escapes me. She's in one piece. Not hurt.

"Oh my God, I was so worried." I whisper into her hair. It smells of dirt and gasoline.

"She's here. Everyone, Ness is here!" I half shout behind me to inform the troops. I don't want to let her out of my arms but she wriggles free, stepping into the hallway. The door falls into its heavy lock. A very sobering sound. Something is happening to Ness.

Beth rushes in from the kitchen, her puffed face lightening. The police officer follows on her heels. Matt must have fallen off the couch and woken up because he stumbles into the foyer in utter disbelief.

"Where were you? You never came back to work. We were searching two blocks for you all night." He asks her. But her face is ghostly. Ness looks from one person to the next before addressing the officer.

"I had a bit of a crazy night." We all try to read her. I'm not sure what to make of it. She looks and sounds so different. Somehow broken. The officer speaks into his walkie and calls off the sear for a missing person we begged them to put into immediate effect.

115

"Calling off the 10-65. Person has been located." After several hours of assuring the police that Ness would never behave in an irrational way, here she is, every bit irrational to me. This is not the woman I know inside and out. It's so confusing and scary. My heart cracks a little. I ignore the deep, physical pang and push through.

Officer hot stuff takes his flashlight and shines it into her pupils.

"Can I have your name and age please?"

She looks at him with confusion. She knows this process better than any of us. She's called so many wellness checks on her own callers, that she could do this police routine herself.

She shakes off her confusion and answers.

"Vanessa Lang, 21. I'm OK. I promise." The flashlight switches off again. I see Ness' face brighten with relief. Like a headache lifting after a few hours of nauseating pain.

"Are you hurt?" The officer continues.

She only shakes her head. We all stare at her, not recognizing the woman who just walked through the front door.

The officer looks between us and our concerned and bewildered faces. He's seen this a million times. A person who never did anything like this, suddenly breaking from the pressures of reality and behaving completely out of turn. He gives my mother-in-law a lopsided smile.

"Settle in. Call us if you need anything." He holds Beth's gaze a tad too long and I refrain from rolling my eyes. Man, pick your moment better. But then he pats me on the shoulder with that weird pity look on his face that says "you're in for a ride" and exits.

The door reveals a bit of daylight. Gloomy again and the clouds have taken over any remanence of sunshine that tried to make a break for it.

"Thank you again" Beth mutters as the officer has already left and we all slowly turn to Ness.

Matt notices something strange in her pocket.

"What is that?" He asks and points.

116

Ness has the gull to roll her eyes and squeezes by us into the kitchen.

We all follow like sheep a strange Shepard and watch her down the remainder of the whiskey straight from the open bottle on the table. She plops the gun on the table. Beth steps back in shock. Now the realization sinks in. She brought a gun home. What happened last night?

Ness scans our faces and dismisses us with sharp words. "Don't worry. There are no more bullets in it." I've never heard that tone from her. Dread is creeping into every fiber of my being.

"Where did you even get this?" I ask. All my fear bundled up in a simple question. Without a blink, she answers and for the first time since I've known her, I know she's lying to me.

"I the alley behind the office."

Matt crosses his arms. "No way."

"What on earth happened to you?" I want to know and fight the urge to shake her or cry.

"I thought I could help someone. Turns out I cannot. I really don't wanna talk about it."

She finishes as though that would be the end of a necessary explanation. All we would ever need to know. Dismissive and short. The Ness that I know would never disrespect anyone like this. She's only ever been rough in a similar way once. That was when her father died and she was in so much pain, that she didn't know how to release any of it. I was there that week. It was hard. I stayed and let her talk to me in a way I normally wouldn't. In a way, she normally wouldn't. This somehow feels similar. What happened? Did someone remind her of her father and it triggered the feeling all over again?

Ness looks around and opens the liquor cabinet. She drinks the first thing she can get her hands on. Makes a face.

"What is this, orange Vodka?" She retches and I finally move into action, just like I did back then. I take the bottle from her and pull out a chair for her to sit.

Matt comes in closer too. Half her friend and half her boss. A very conflicting mixture right now.

"Did you meet one of our callers outside of work? Id that where you got the gun?"

Ness sighs, not planning on answering anyone. So Matt continues, his voice breaking with worry.

"What the fuck, Ness. We have rules for a reason."

She snaps. Her sharp eyes awake and piercing.

"I know. I wrote the fucking rules.

Everything within me balls together in more fears. She's about to break. I'm about to break.

"Who were you with? Who is this client?" I ask and feel her judgment towards me. She scoffs, as though I have no right to even ask that question.

"Calm down, please. I'll explain later."

And with that, I boil over.

"I'm concerned. You're acting crazy." As the word leaves my lips, I know it will just fuel whatever fire is stirring within her. But some part of me needs it to. She's hurting me. Hurting all of us.

"Crazy? I do one unexpected thing that doesn't fit your image of me and I'm crazy?" She snaps at me shaking her head. There are dark, crusted speckles of what looks like blood on her clothes. Luckily my thoughts are interrupted when Beth comes closer. She tries to touch Ness' hand.

"Honey, you were missing for a whole night and came back with a gun in your pocket." Her voice is amazingly steady. She's a fantastic mother. That patience and restraint is the most admirable thing I've ever seen.

But Ness still doesn't want to give us an inch.

"I tried to help someone. It didn't work. No one got hurt and we can all go back to our normal, predictable lives."

Ness reaches and manages to grab the vodka bottle from me. She takes another big gulp before I can take it away from me again. Anger is bubbling up in me. Pure and simple. Does she not know what this does to all of us? This fear and worry?

"What the fuck are you doing?" I ask. My anger shines through dominantly in every word. Let it.

"I'm numbing myself. I always do everything right. Always. School, job, perfect relationship, perfect trajectory. So you can forgive me one night."

Beth blinks and in that motherly tone tells her: "Let's calm down a bit. I'll make us all some tea-"

Ness isn't having it and looks her straight in the eyes.

"Everyone stop and get off my ass!"

We all freeze as though she slapped us across the face. Beth tries to cover her hurt, but I see it. I want to give her a hug.

"I'm not your little Barbie doll. You don't have to tell me what to think and how to behave and condescend to me when I tap out of line. I'm perfectly capable of making my own decisions and owning my own mistakes."

Sobering words from a girl who is much less than. I watch Matt shake his head in confusion and pick up his jacket.

"I'll get out of your hair." He muffles to us and his glance barely meets mine. He's scared of getting his head bitten off by this poisonous viper in our midst. I don't blame him. I have half a mind to join him and go get some breakfast. But I love this woman in front of me. And sometimes you have to double down and fight for the people you love. Especially when they are too weak to fight for themselves.

As he leaves, Ness calls after him. "I'll see you at work." He turns and keeps his eyes on the floor.

"Take tonight off. I think you need it."

She smiles. A lethal thing without kindness.

"Case in point. Another person who knows what's best for me."

Beth's expression turns solemn as Matt leaves. She had raised her daughter much better than this. Full of kindness and consideration. Two words not associated with this morning in any way, shape, or form.

"I'm gonna go to bed." Ness exclaims after a moment and leaves Beth and me alone in our confusion.

119

I rub my face. Trying to figure out what storm just came over us. This night sits in my bones. I'm exhausted.

"Hun, don't worry too much about it. She loves you. She's probably just a bit shaken." Beth chimes and draws soothing circles on my back with the palm of her hand. She doesn't deserve the treatment her daughter gave her. Not at all.

I don't know what makes me say it, but I blurt it out.

"I bought a ring last week."

Beth smirks. "I know."

My eyes dart to her in surprise.

"Ness saw you hide it. You're not the most subtle person on the planet."

My shoulders droop. She saw it. I knew it. I knew it scared her. Marriage, her father's death. All of it. I feel like a fool. With a suddenness envied by a bullet, I feel partially responsible for tonight's outbursts. All within seconds.

"That explains the outburst. She's never really dated anyone else. Maybe it's cold feet." I say out loud and rationalize my love's roughness.

Beth only nods, comforting me with her presence.

I know what I need to do. I can fix this. I know I can. Fixing things is my specialty.

"I'll go talk to her." I say with hope and conviction as I rise.

"Maybe give her a moment to cool down?" Beth suggests, but I'm already on my way. Ready.

"It's ok. I got this." I tell her, kiss her soft cheek and head up the stairs, my heart much lighter.

CHAPTER 24: TIME TO BREATHE - NESS

This entire night made me feel heavy. I pace even though there isn't much room for that. My attic room is small and feels more like a cage at present. Stuffy and dark. The bed in the corner immediately makes its presence known when my knee connects with the bedpost. I know it'll become a nasty bruise, but at this moment in time, I hardly notice the sting it gives me.

My head is spinning and recounts all of the crazy bits and pieces that made this night an adventure and a nightmare. Was it real? Any of it?

I shut my eyes willing short breaths of air into my lungs. A flash of ice-blue eyes shoots across my vision and I almost hyperventilate. This isn't working.

I sit down on the bed and feel the comforter fabric. So soft and welcoming. I pull the thick blanket over my shoulders. Something broke within me. That moment Grace called, something changed irreparably.

I've never before given one of my regular callers to anyone else. Especially not Emma. I know how fragile she is. I like her and care about her. I shake my head at myself. I just handed her to the new kid without a second thought. What is wrong with me? I hope she'll forgive me. I slump down a little more, pulling the blanket tighter around me.

I just left. Grace showed up and I just followed her. The guilt is overwhelming. The entire night was so exhilarating and strange, that I didn't spare a single thought for my mother or Luke. I feel sick to my stomach. I love them both. They're truly warm and kind-hearted humans and I just left without a care.

I feel the heavy tear building and don't stop it as it breaks from my lower lashes and carves its way across my cheek. Somewhere near my nose, it ebbs. I don't deserve them. I take another deep breath and try to shake off the self-pity. But it's not working.

The next thought is even more nauseating. Grace and I kissed. Twice.

I lick my lips as if I can still feel her on them. Her cool, soft, pillowy shape. Like a drug. A small whimper escapes my throat.

I force my eyes open again. I kissed another person. I know Luke loves me; wants to marry me and give me everything I could possibly ever want. But I kissed someone else. And even though Grace is dead, I can't stop thinking about her. She's dead.

That's the next thought in my mind and the images of her falling through the roof and her body landing far below flash across my mind. She was wide-eyed. Expectant and wild. Ready. The second time she embraced death with such...well...grace.

A small chuckle escapes me at the wordplay. She's dead. Heavy resolve settles within me and another tear replaces the first. I barely knew her. So why am I feeling this confusing and strange cocktail of emotions? I was happy. My life was perfect. It's better without her in it. And yet...

The next thought makes me shudder. I brought a gun home. An antique revolver. Only due to Luke's quick thinking, the police didn't see it. I'll have to thank him later. If I can ever look him in the eyes again. My friends and family are patient and wonderfully tolerant, but I'll have to answer those questions sooner than later. How? Do I tell them the truth?

"Hey guys, sorry about last night. I met this vampire girl and followed her into the night. She really wanted to die, so I thought I'd help her out and give it a shot."

I snort. My sense of humor is not what it used to be. It's darkened over the past few nights.

I'm leaking tears and somehow I can't stop crying. How do I tell them anything? I can't, can I? Do I tell Luke that I kissed a stranger? He'd be heartbroken.

So many thoughts. I can't even begin to organize any of them. But I know, I can't say a word. Grace is dead and I'm grieving. My heart is heavy and I have to carry that all by myself.

A knock on the door startles me into sitting upright.

Luke opens the door slightly. I hear it in his hesitation.

"I really need some space right now." I tell him, trying to sound as steady as I possibly can. But as the words come out, I hear my voice break.

But I see his fluffy hair bounce past the door. He's coming in whether I want to talk or not. It's not fair to push him away. I know that. BUT what do I tell him?

He just stands there, looking at me awkwardly. So handsome. So sweet and boyishly insecure when presented with the female waves of emotional outbursts.

"Who is this client?" He asks, trying his very best to sound unafraid of the question.

He has every right to every question. But I really don't want to speak.

"Let's chat tomorrow? I'm not feeling well." I wipe my tears off my face.

"Did you cheat on me?" The words just tumble from him and before I think I shout.

"No!"

Lier, my inner voice picks at me. And it's true. I kissed Grace. Twice. I would have kissed her again and again and again. I did cheat. With my heart and my lips. But what good does telling him that do? I can't explain this. I can't hurt him and then not explain this. I don't even know why I did it.

He exhales in relief and closes the door behind him, worry edged on his beautiful face. He sits down next to me and hugs me, comforter included in the most awkward way imaginable. I really don't want him near me at the moment, but he starts wiping and kissing my tears away and I don't want to hurt him more than I already have either. What right do I have to cause this wonderful man any more pain?

I try to wriggle free. Suddenly the warm blanket has become a hard shackle around me. Too hot. Clammy.

"I really need you to let me in. I can help you, you know?" He whispers in my ear and starts kissing my neck just under it. The sensation makes me shudder. He is encouraged by that reaction although that is not what my body is trying to signal him.

I turn to him to tell him, but before I can form the words, his lips are on mine. Hard and claiming. Searching for an answer to every question of the night. Easing his fear of losing me. His hands palm my cheeks on either side and he kisses me again. Deeply.

Finally, he comes up for air.

"This isn't really the right time." I say the words but I see tears sprouting on his lashes too. My heart breaks.

I can do this I tell myself and close my eyes for the next kiss. His tongue explores my own and a flash of ice-blue eyes burrows its way through my mind. I can't stop it.

I relax a bit into Luke's need to claim me physically. Another kiss. Softer this time. But my mind isn't with him. My hands feel his hair but my heart turns it blonde and luscious.

"I've got you, always. I'll protect you no matter what." He says as his salty tears fall into my mouth. I nod, placating him as best as possible. I would love for his words to be true. But there are things this kind man can not protect me from. Meeting a vampire, real or not, having shot a gun and tried to kill, real or not, having a broken heart, real or not and not being able to share any of it. He always tries to fix things. It's sweet, but sometimes not helpful.

When my father died he used this phrase of getting 'past' it. I couldn't explain to him that I would never want to 'get past it'. Past my father. I was grieving and my father and his death would always be a part of me. So will Grace.

More tears stream down my cheek and now we're crying in unison.

Luke kisses me again and takes off his shirt. His skin is golden and his body is sculpted just right. I run a finger slowly over his collar bone. In my mind's eye, the skin is pearl-white and cool to the touch. Soft.

He shoves us with urgent need under the blankets and fights with the buttons of my pants. I don't resist but I also don't help him.

"I'm not really-" I start and look him in the eyes.

"I need to be inside you right now." He whispers, the desperation and pain too overwhelming for me to say much else.

My underwear joins his own on the floor as he finally claims me.

"It's how I feel connected to you." He stutters clumsily and I just hold him. I love him but I'm in the middle of an emotional storm I cannot navigate. So I do the one thing that feels calming.

I close my eyes yet again and let my mind go. Slowly it drifts. Blonde, long hair. Arching eyebrows and those elegantly curved lips. I think of her with him inside of me. It feels like another betrayal.

"I love you so much, you have no idea." He whispers and it sounds like a sputtering candle about to be extinguished.

We rock back and forth. The most steady part of my night. But I am in no way present.

Another thought passes by. Grace dissolves into ashes. First her delicate fingers, her arms; then her hair on the breeze, and finally, her smile. I see myself holding onto her until there's nothing more to hold.

I feel Luke's body shuddering in sweet release. One of us finds it. After a few heaving breaths, he settles into an unyielding hold and falls asleep within a minute. I can barely breathe. Tear stream openly down the sides of my face as I stare flatly at the ceiling. After a long time of crying and feeling so alone and yet, not alone enough, I exhaust myself enough to drift off. Not a good sleep, but pitch black nonetheless.

CHAPTER 25: EMPTY

At some point, Luke finally leaves. I'm dazed and only feel the cold air engulfing my body more fully. His weight is gone and I feel the relief of one deep, unencumbered breath. Sweat still sticks to my torso and tears to my cheeks. He kisses my lips, but I pretend to sleep through it.

Let him leave.

When the door closes, I feel better. I gulp. I've loved Luke for such a long time. He really knows every part of me and loves me regardless of any flaws. He's seen me become an adult. He was there when my father died and my life fell apart. And now, I can't even share with him what happened last night.

My eyes flutter open. I feel gross, whether from guilt or lying in sweat and not sleeping, I do not know.

After a shower, I feel better. I just stood there for almost forty minutes, letting the steaming water pummel me into a state of peace. Now I still feel guilty and awful, but also clean. I have no more sense of time. The hazy light outside doesn't help much either. Perpetual clouds make it hard to distinguish morning from noon and evening. My alarm clock reads 6 pm. The light starts already fading behind the thick clouds as the street lamps spark to life.

I lie back down. Exhaustion spreads through every bone and I drift off. A flash of an image spreads across my mind again. It's familiar. It's Grace's beautiful face in the palm of my hand and it slowly fades to dust.
I hear a knock. Somewhere distant. A knock?

I look around in the dream. Grace is gone. The dust glitters through the rays of light streaming in from the broken window. I look up. The fallen roof shows the spot where Grace fell.

Another knock. Much more incessant.

I'm still in my dream with no intention of waking. The dust whips around in the wind. Strange shapes and curves. It's pretty. It solidifies into a pair of ice-blue eyes. So familiar. They change to silver. My heart skips a beat. Excitement flushes through me from head to toe. Grace.

Another knock. Repeating.
Finally, I sit up straight and open my eyes. What is that sound? Then I realize. The window. The knock is real and coming from the window. A shiver runs down my spine and I know before I even turn my head. I don't believe it. I don't really dare to believe it. But the knocking continues. I rise to my bare feet in nothing but my towel. My wet hair is still heavy with water and not in its most curly shape.

There she is. Hovering on the roof like a cat. Almost casual. Her hood mostly covering her shiny, blonde tresses, but they peak through. She places her hand on the glass. I still don't believe it. My hand touches the same spot on the window on my side. The cold seeps into my skin. Startling.

"You sleep like the dead." She says and it sounds a little muffled through the glass.
"The irony." She smirks and I trace the shape of her fingers, leaving watery trails on the window.

She cocks her head to the side. Like a bird. It's beautiful and scary at the same time.
"Are you going to open? You're being rude."
I am still not sure whether this is part of my guilt-filled dream-state or reality.
"I saw you die." I state remembering ash.

Grace smirks. "Actually, you saw me die twice and the second time was not very pleasant at all."

"I thought you were gone." I state and my voice breaks.

I study her ethereal face and the delicate column of her nose. My fingers trace her lips. Longing building within me. I know what they feel like. Taste like. But only on my own lips. Without a thought, I suck in my own bottom lip and heat flushes to my cheeks. Grace catches the change in my mood.
"Open the window."
I look at her. Resisting.
"You're not real."

She lightly knocks against the glass with her open palm. Half growling as she speaks. Guttural. "Open the window, or I will."
I move very slowly. "Don't you have to be invited in?"
Her eyebrows rise in question.
"Garlic, bats, crucifixes. But this one is the silliest of all of the vampire troves. Helpful though, I must say. Now open the damn window."

I unlatch the little lock and step back. Heat is pooling in my core. The kind that makes it hard to think straight.

The window doors swing inwards and Grace looks me up and down. Her eyes glazing over when they find the spot where the heat accumulates with more and more determination.

"Not real?" She asks.
I hold my ground.
"No. Everyone knows vampires aren't real."
With cat-like smoothness, Grace swoops in and plunges her lips onto my mouth. Tongue exploring softly, but with confidence. A dance. A game. I open for her. Feel

her and tease her lips with my own tongue. Exploring every small dip. So slowly.

A moan escapes me and surprises us both. I blink and my quick lashes bend against Grace's cool skin. She smirks and answers with a kiss, her hand bending my head to her will, her lips parting my own. She takes and I give willingly.

"Not real at all." I whisper.

I let my fingers explore her back. Like marble. I try my best not to be shy, to switch off my head and let my heart and body guide me. But I'm a little nervous, and my fingertips hitch a bit when they glide over the smooth surface of her muscled shoulder.
Grace angles us towards my bed and my heart jumps all the way into my throat. She pauses and looks at me. Deeply. A question. Do I want this?

Her nostrils flare slightly. "Your room still smells like him." She says and frowns.
Is that jealousy? I almost smile and my confidence returns.
I kiss her, playfully. Just a small flick of my tongue. It works like oil on fire. Her eyes spark up in that shiny silver.
"I don't particularly like smelling someone else near you." My hand traces her sternum. "Then change it." I tell her.

Her eyes glow. It's mesmerizing.
I don't know why but I have to touch her sensuous mouth. Carefully, I part those pillowy lips. There, small and sharp, her lethal canines. The end of many lives just above the flesh of my finger. Beautiful.

I lean closer and Grace doesn't pull away when I kiss each one gently. Just my lips. I pull back again and look at her entirely.

"Do that again." She orders and I oblige. My thumb parts her teeth and she bites it gently. A small sting of temporary pain spreads through my hand reminding me just how alive I am. Exhilarating. I let the tip of my tongue glide over her teeth, exploring. Grace shudders with restraint.

With steady hands, Grace undoes the loose knot of my towel. It falls to the floor and I stand before her as I am. Naked. For a split second, I feel the cold chill in the room. Eyes locked on mine, Grace gently scratches down with a fingernail. She starts at my collarbone. The nails leave a soft red trace behind and chase away any thought of coldness. Heat throbs through my chest and pools further down, making me twitch in hidden places. It's joined by raised peach-fuzz hair. I arch towards the caress, mind emptying entirely.

This is real.

I let myself fall backward onto my bed and watch Grace without a sliver of shyness as she takes off her own clothes, buckle by buckle. She unlatches the restraints of her leather gauntlets around her wrists holding hidden knives in place. Curved and terrifying. She drops her pants too and each layer reveals more weapons. All small, sharp knives of different shapes. Like a surgeon's briefcase hidden all over her body. Finally, after what feels like one hundred scalpels later, she too is nude.

Her body is perfect. Each curve made from decades of fighting. Lean muscle, feminine, soft, but lethal nonetheless. I can't take my eyes off of her. She stands before me, not a stitch of clothing. Not a single scar anywhere.

131

Suddenly I feel a bit small in front of her. I do have things about my own body I'd rather change. With a swift motion, I grab the blanket and drag it across my stomach. Grace smiles and with the elegance of a dancer joins me under the blanket, a kiss on my lips and a hand in my damp hair.

I feel her body entirely entangled with mine. Cold and strong. I shiver a bit and to her delight, my own body rises to her touch. She toys with that reaction and repeats it like a cat.

The kisses become even deeper, and I let my own fingers rove across wherever they please.

Her thighs are velvet-covered steel. I marvel at the sensation. Then my fingers wander towards her inner thighs, a bit softer, and I hold my touch just below where she wants it. I can feel her own need as she grinds into me in slow waves of hip to mouth. Writhing against the opposite movement from me.

"Bite me. I want it." I whisper. And I feel her golden-haired head lowering to the skin below my chest. I feel her smile against me.
"No." She says simply and nips at the side of my belly button.
"Please." I beg her and Grace pauses coming back up to face me.
"Never. But I'd like you to beg some more." Grace says and parts my knees with the steady hand of a lover who's done this for centuries.
I give in.

CHAPTER 26: THEN IT ALL CHANGED

We've been dozing in and out of a satisfied slumber for a few hours. Just calm and entangled in each other's naked bodies. Or at least I've been slumbering. I don't know whether Grace can. Does she sleep? Does she need to?

The thoughts sober me up a little bit out of the beautiful lull of sex. Her body felt almost human. So soft, lean, and muscled in most places, curvy and full in others. I sigh.

But she's not human, no matter how much she is made to fool anyone into believing otherwise.

I blink and the movement against the dip of her shoulder makes Grace shift with a small huff of a chuckle. I want to ask but I swallow the question down. How stupid would it sound out loud? Do you sleep?

But she must have felt something change in my behavior and kisses the top of my head as she plays with my hair.

"What is it?" She asks lowly. In that sweet, scratchy, lazy voice that's almost a whisper.

I shake my head and she tries to angle my head to make me look at her. But I burrow down a bit further into the corner of her neck.

"Now you're shy?" She muses and I can hear a smirk forming on her sinful lips.

I don't know why the question passes my lips. It has nothing to do with sleep, but I blurt it out before I think it through.

"Do you still want to die?" It feels like the air around us freezes. My heart thumps heavy and half of me is so afraid of the answer.

With gentle fingers, Grace strokes the lobe of my ear. So loving. For a long moment, way too long, she says nothing.

Finally, I angle my eyes towards hers and search for an answer I already know deep down.

"Yes." She whispers and my heart breaks a bit. My breath quickens and I feel the need to 'fix it'. Fix what? I ask myself. This beautiful being is already dead, kills others, and ISN'T REAL.

"You didn't enjoy -" With a tender, feather-light finger, she interrupts my foolish question and kisses the tip of my nose. It tickles slightly and makes it bunch up.
"I loved every second of it." She says and in her eyes, I can read the solid truth behind those words. A small part of me settles.

But a much bigger part of me doesn't understand. We have something. It's a magnetic force that drew us to each other. Into each other. I've known this beautiful woman for what? Two days? Nights? Somehow within that short timeframe, I've thrown away every anchor to my perfect life, for her. To be with her to experience her and breathe her in. I need her. There's an existential bond between us that I cannot explain. When you have feelings like that, why on earth would you still want to go? She seems to be reading my thoughts as though I'd spoken them out loud.
"I'd still be alone tomorrow, or the next day, or when you get so scared I'd accidentally harm you."
I pull myself up a bit further on the bed to fully face her. She's thinking it through. We can find a solution.
"I don't think you would ever do that." I say that with such confidence. Of someone, I've just met. Of a being, I don't fully understand.
"Or you'd age and die and I'd be alone then too. Always the same ending." The words hang in the thick air, heavy and solemn.

Both of us know where this discussion will go and yet, I ask the next question without hesitation. Ready to change myself, give myself up entirely.
"What if you bite me? Turn me immortal?
She smiles. But I know this particular smile. My mother has it and it doesn't reach her eyes.
"Even if I knew how I wouldn't wish this upon you. Having to kill. It changes you."

134

And there it is. Another person who makes decisions for me. A plume of anger rises in my stomach. I am a grown woman. I don't need my loved ones to plan out my life, tell me what's the best route and prevent me from taking my own path.

"You don't know how? Biting doesn't work?" I hear the change in my tone and sit up.

Grace remains calm. Understanding. One of her fingers idly traces the peach fuzz on my lower back. It's annoyingly soothing.

"I've tried. Biting, giving blood. Nothing. I cannot die and I cannot give immortality."

Somehow her calm honesty is infuriating. I don't want to lose her. I think I love her.

Dread. Pure dread at the thought and the vulnerability that opens me up to, streams through my veins. I try to mask it, but I can barely swallow. My voice changes.

"How did you turn?" The words hitch but make it out.

Grace's touch turns more comforting. The palm of her hand replaces the single finger. Cool, gentle circles.

"My father did something I will never completely understand.

All I remember are flashes here and there. Blood too. Not sure if it was mine, or his."

The thought of her story. The fire, her family burning alive. It sobers me a bit, but not enough to prevent the first, heavy tear from tumbling from my lashes. She continues.

"And then I remember hunger. Pain. Bone deep. Chills. I changed. I bit him. Tore. Liked it." She halts for a moment. Giving me time to process this. She bit her own father. A person she deeply loved. Loves still. I don't want to empathize and understand, but part of me does. Of course, she doesn't want this for me. Turning me or hurting me. Another tear joins the first one and I try my best to hold back, but my body starts shaking from deep inside.

"I remember drinking. Seeing his dead body when I came to. There was fire. Everywhere. In huge swallowing waves. We burned. And then the next night I woke up in a pile of rubble and my father was gone." She stops as I start to let go of my own control and cry openly. With a soft motion, she sits up to scoop my head back into her arms and lay us back down together. My tears covering us both in wet salt. She kisses my forehead and continues to soothe me. Anger, shame, fear, love, all of those emotions battle within me at the same time and I have no idea which one is prevailing its dominance. I'm a mess.

"Maybe it's connected. You taking and giving life." I force it out. Not sure why.

"Maybe." She agrees.

My desperation wins the battle within me. "What are we gonna do? I want more of this. I don't want to let you go. I feel excited with you. Alive."

Soft lips start kissing away each new tear. It breaks my heart some more.

"I don't want you to die." I croak.

"You need me to die." She tells me and I know it's true. But I don't want it to be.

My body convulses with sobs more and more violently, giving my heart some space. I love her. The realization hits me to the core. I love Grace and my love won't be enough to sustain us. My love won't fix this. Nothing can. Grace holds me, kisses me, and loves me in her own way. Closeness and tenderness.

All of a sudden, Grace's eyes widen. A sudden inhale of air.

"What is it?" I ask, watching her eyes sparkle silver in the dim light. Something happened and it has nothing to do with our conversation.

Grace jumps out of bed. Her nostrils flare. Her pupils dilate. The blue around turning entirely silver.

I pull the blanket closer around me. The sudden chill makes my ears ring.

Grace pulls her pants on and hastily tugs her shirt over her head. She pulls out the metal gauntlets and fastens the buckles with a warrior's efficiency. Her father's hand-crafted finger scalpel shines like her eyes. A deadly, shiny claw.

The window. Her attention is fully fixed on the window. My own eyes dart towards it but I can't see anything.

I rise, still drained and sleepy from the emotional toll of this night.

"What's happening?" I ask her and wipe the remaining tears off my cheeks.

"I don't know. Stay here." She sounds demanding. Like an officer of some sort. An authority that doesn't sit well with me at this particular moment.

"I will not." I tell her, hackles raised, ready to argue.

Vicious, more animal than human, Grace turns. Eyes silver, teeth shining.

"Stay." She orders and the demand freezes me solid. Grace is equally frightening and beautiful. She opens the window and pops herself through.

I've never dressed so quickly. Pants, socks, a sweater. Whatever lies on the floor. One eye is always on the open window. Cold air rushes in and slams into me with waking force.

Grace stands on the shingles. Barefoot, the cold not bothering her immortal body. Each movement is full predator, smooth, and ready. A breeze plays with her hair. Her nostrils flare imperceptibly. Whatever she's picking up, it's worrying her. Her eyebrows bunch together and she scans the darkness ahead. The fog, impenetrable to my human eyes.

There. Her head stops cold, having found something in the mist.

She stares into the street. Slick. Frost covers part of it. Shiny.

I venture out onto the roof behind her. A bit louder. The shingles creek under my feet. I squint and try to make out what she sees, but the movement unsettles my balance and I waver.

She whips her head around and implores me. "Please go back inside. It's not safe." Still a bit on edge, my first instinct is to bark a retort. But there's movement in the shadows across the street and I can feel something being very, very off.

"What do you mean?" I ask her unnecessarily. Both of us staring into the same nothingness.

There. Grace's eyes land on it. Her pupils pulsate once. She exhales in surprise.

A dark figure, tall and imposing stands looking back at us. I recognize its form, its broad shoulders and long, strange hands with nails sharpened to sting. Fear builds within me, replacing the turmoil in the pit of my stomach. It's the figure from the elevator in the aquarium. His long fingers held the door open for me. With ancient politeness. He's dressed funny. A suit. Simple but of an old style. With nimble fingers, he switches a shiny blade through the air. Skill. It catches the light.

Grace's breath becomes a cloud in the cold air. Knowing hits both of us to the core. I ask anyway.

"Who is that?"

Grace guides me back to the window, protective and worried.

"Someone like me." She says and my face releases any doubt of my rising fear. She whips her head back to the figure in the street who seems to be waiting for her. Taunting her with his shiny blade.

"For your own safety go back inside and lock the doors." She begs. Her tone isn't demanding. It's not to try to condescend or know better than I do. So I nod. I squeeze her hand and she understands my ask. She leans down and kisses me once more. Deeply. Urgency and dread on her lips.

Then the kiss releases, our hands unlock and I feel cold air where her touch has been. I watch her stalk to the edge of the roof and shout after her.

"Are you not coming?"

In utter disbelief and shock, Grace breathes over her shoulder towards me, one last twinkle of those silver, starry eyes towards me. "I always thought I was the only one."
Then she jumps down to follow the stranger into the night."

CHAPTER 27: NO RETURN

I close the French doors on the little window and blink, taking a beat. So many emotions to sort through that I don't know where to begin. So I decide to postpone sorting altogether and do something useful. Grace is following an immortal creature. Something she doesn't know nor fully understand. As I hop into my pants, one clumsy leg at a time, fear strikes me and strikes deep. What if that tall man isn't like her? What if he's dangerous?

But I push the idea aside. Grace is immortal. We've established that most thoroughly against my better judgment. Twice.

She'll be fine. However, I'm not so sure I can say the same about myself. I love her. And even though she might not be able to make me immortal herself, she's not the only death-impaired being I know. I know another. Sparkly and full of electric fire. I wonder just how far Luke's research has progressed and if he's found anything useful. Well, checking his notes for myself seems like a much better use of my time than sulking around my room, waiting for Grace to return, or not to return at all...

The thought sends an ice-cold shiver down my spine. I shake it off and put on a sweater and a beanie. It's cold outside. Another glance at the window confirms that. Small ice crystals build in formation on the glass. But I pay them no heed. I'm full of adrenaline and won't feel the cold on my skin. Nevertheless, I put on a pair of thick socks and good hiking shoes, and this night promises more adventures.

When I finally close the door to my room, something feels strange... as if I'm leaving a part of my old life behind. Having made a final decision. A step towards the unknown, right off a cliff. I hesitate, my hand still on the door handle. The warmth of the house surrounds me with love. I felt love here. My family's love. My father died here and my mother continued living just for me. Even with only half her smile left.

As much as I respect and adore her for it, I'm afraid of that fate. I don't want to inherit her half-smile and a broken heart. I have to follow mine. I have to find a solution and be with Grace. Something else flares up within me. Hope.

But the door across from me opens as well and my mom stumbles out half asleep towards me. Familiar eyes search my own and I gulp under the scrutiny.

"You're up late, or awake very, very early, darling." She wipes her face with one hand, looking a little more worn than usual. My mother is a beautiful woman, but that's never the quality people first notice about her. The thought makes me smile.

"I'm going to the aquarium. I have to talk to Luke." It's not a lie. I know I can't lead that wonderful man on when I know what my heart desires more than anything. But hearing my voice say it out loud, feels so different. A small sliver of panic shoots through my chest.

She looks me over again, sadness building up in her face as if she already knows. My wise, wonderful mother is so incredibly intuitive. She nods.

"Be gentle." Her voice remains steady, even though her face betrays its intent. Gentle. What a word.

Is that what I should be? Or would it be much kinder to rip off the Band-Aid? The different options and possible outcomes race through my head, each terrible and heartbreaking in its own way. Luke deserves none of them, nor any of what I already did to him last night. I feel rotten. Through and through. Guilty and dirty and altogether awful. My mother reads that on my face too and crosses the distance between us. Her arms wrap around me before I can stop her and she kisses my cheek. "He...we only ever wanted you to be happy. Remember that."

Her breath warms my ear as she says it and the words ring true. She means my father of course.

The man I still strive to be so perfect for even though he'll never know. I wonder what he would think of my adventure, of Grace. Would he welcome this? Be worried? Be as petrified and excited as I am? He would want me to be happy. He loved Luke, sure, but happiness is messy. It can take turns and lead you to a completely different destination than you originally set out for. I remember Dad telling me to take happy moments wherever I could find them, cherish and celebrate them, and laugh often and hard. Some of the guilt melts away and I feel better. Even now, as an adult, my mom has this wonderful ability to calm me down with a few, sincere words of love.

I lean back a bit and let her see the small spots of mist building up in the corners of my eyes. I don't bother to wipe them away. She smiles a bit. On her face, I see another thought building, but she holds back, unsure whether to give it words or not.

"What is it?" I prod, not in the mood for patience. She shakes her head, not wanting to continue and destroy the tender moment we just had. But this is my mother we're talking about and she cannot help herself.

"You know you're different?" Her voice comes out straight, but it's put on. Her parental training of keeping a serious topic light on purpose.

I smile. "Yes. I think I'm finding something new about myself." I share without hesitation. A bit of my anxiety has lifted. It feels a bit freer somehow.

"I feel like I can breathe better, clearer." I continue explaining and my mother nods.

"That's wonderful, darling. Just promise me one thing." She holds as I adjust my beanie, ready to head to the lab and search for answers. I look at her, expectant and a bit sheepish. What promise is she about to coax out of me? To be safe? Well, I'd certainly have to lie about that, wouldn't I? Be careful? Also a tough one at this very moment in time. Be honest? I've really outdone myself on the basics the last couple of days.

But her voice is calm and gentle. "Don't forget your heart." It stops me. I don't know what to tell her. So I just nod. I lean down a bit and kiss her forehead, swallowing down the doubts and fears that are gripping tightly onto every cell of my being. But I will listen to her, not forgetting my heart, not being a coward.

I walk down the stairs, acutely aware of the groaning wood. Somehow, living here all these years, I'm hearing it consciously for the first time. Like I'm coming to life.

The night outside is fresh and crisp, but for once, it's thankfully not raining. I am exhilarated. I can hardly pull my mittens on fast enough over quickly stiffening fingers. I am going to find a solution. My mother supports my happiness. I will figure this out. Maybe it's as simple as being stung by a small, immortal, electric jellyfish. I mount the bike and glance back at my house, giving my old life a small smile as I race into the night.

Speeding through the dark, I wonder what would happen if I told Luke about Grace. What she is. I wonder what would win out, his jealousy or his curiosity and obsession with finding a cure for death. I know the answer and that makes me breathe just a little bit easier. He would choose to know every piece of the puzzle. Every intricate little sliver. He'd pick that over me in a heartbeat.

Shame sparks up in me as I look for justifications and flaws in our bond. His thirst for knowledge has very little to do with my own reasons for having to, wanting to end our relationship. I sigh, letting air escape my lungs in a long burst. The thought is very clear now. Not just a question anymore. It makes it real. I have to break things off with Luke. My best friend. A bit of my heart.

The cold envelopes me and finds little sneaky ways to slither through my layers of clothing. Is that what my mother meant? To not forget my heart?

Luke will always have a piece of it. No matter what. I pedal faster, letting the hill burn the muscle in my thighs. The pain brings me back to reality and presence. I see the blue light of the aquarium against the misty pre-dawn

Atlanta sky. Like a gem. The glow it emanates is beautiful and calming.

I drive around back. I can't exactly walk through the front door with my endeavor. Extracting information on Luke's favorite little jellyfish buddy will require some serious delicacy.

I hide my bike in the adjacent parking lot. Luckily, there are always a few RVs parked in it. After the pandemic, many people chose to live there and forgo rent. I don't blame them. The big shadows are perfect for me. No security guard, however friendly, can spot me tonight. There is no solid explanation for what I am about to do.

I weave through the cars and fences to the back door of the aquarium. This is where the trashcans and delivery docks are. Every morning, this place gets tons of fish. It's smelly and in a perpetual state of wetness and slime. I see the metal trash containers and I hide between them to scope out the backdoor. I know they usually leave it ajar around this time of night. The camera above faces the loading dock, where the delivery drivers come in and out. No one would know this, but it's angled off and I have George to thank for this little bit of information. It doesn't see the second door, next to the recycling bin. They adjusted the cameras a little while back because some of the young pickup drivers tried to steal a dolphin for fun. They made it all the way to the seal exhibit, broke the glass, and passed out face down in a bunch of seal dung. They were arrested, of course. There are some very strange people out there. But thanks to those fools, I know this lovely, little loophole and I can use it to my advantage. Now both the back cameras focus only on the docks. My spot is safe.

I wait for a moment and spy the small piece of paper the whale trainers leave in the lock at my door to keep it propped open. This fortress has one flaw; humans. The trainers here have their own hierarchy and coolness scale. Apparently smoking like a European in the 80s has made a recent comeback and this is the place to be. Cigarette butts litter the ground like stars in the night sky and the door is always unlocked.

All this fancy security and this is what makes all the difference.

I pop out from between the containers and without much trouble, I pull the door. It opens for me.

CHAPTER 28: DEVILS AND DEMONS - GRACE

If my heart could pound, it would. It would beat so loudly that one could use it to accompany music. Fast-paced and vivacious. For hundreds of years, I have been this immortal thing, this version of a human but not a human, I've never met anyone like me. Not once. I've searched of course. There was a period in the late 1800's when travel became commonplace enough even for women, I went all across the country.

With stolen money, I hired a young, human governess and a male driver and paid them so outlandishly well that any absurdities were first overlooked, and later accepted. Harriet was the girl's name and I remember her fondly. She was only twenty-four and well-educated given her economic status. She didn't come from money and I found her in Brooklyn. Her mother had tried to bargain her off to an uptown brothel keeper but I took her instead. I paid her to fill in the gaps that I had already forgotten about human behavior. To my surprise, there were many. Then we went about hiring the right driver. Someone kind and quiet. Someone who could be bought, but also wouldn't sell me out at the first opportunity. My first try failed. The man drove us for a week in the old carriage, down to Charleston and Savannah. But on the second week, he drank his fill and then some and tried to force himself on Harriet in the little inn we were staying at. In their salon of all places, filled with a few other laughing men.
It happened so fast that I still don't remember the details, but I tore him to shreds. His limbs from his wretched body. I covered the velvet, Victorian furniture in his blood, and the ceiling dripping with gore. I have a vague flash in my mind of the other men stopping their amusement and staring at me as though they had just met a ghost. I suppose they did. I killed them too. More involuntary but most welcome financial donations to our cause. When I was done, drunk on their blood and my

147

rage silent again, I found myself staring into Harriet's surprised face. She stood near the fireplace holding someone's hand. A slave man, tall, with kind eyes. His brown skin beaded with sweat near the heat of the fire. He handed me his handkerchief and the deal was set.

I don't know why I knew I could trust them both, but I just did. His name was John. I paid them both equally and we became close. By day they listened in the cafes and salons on my behalf, for stories of devils and demons. First, we were in the South and there were many such tales. Every city had a myth of someone like me. A bloodthirsty creature who would come around at night and eat only virgins. I roll my eyes at the thought. Oh, the idea of virginity being the purest form of femininity to love and adore. To me, it always appeared rather boring with a heap of emotional responsibilities following the act. But back in the day, people had even stranger ideas about women than they do now.

When word spread of the wealthy heiress and her young governess, we were invited to many social outings, my youth and beauty being as much of a reason as the curiosity of my upbringing and breeding.

The first few times we heard a tale of a monster, I got excited and listened intently to every gruesome detail. I wanted to know who and what I was. I wanted to know what secret my father held all those years and where he came from. The good doctor Lucard never told me. But the stories were empty. Old wives' tales spun to scare young women into a shudder as an excuse to offer a jacket or a warm arm if she felt scandalous.

There was a summer party on a plantation home just outside of Savannah when such a story was told to me. A young man offered me his arm on a walk and I took it, enjoying the night's breeze on the mile-long trail below the Spanish moss-covered trees. I'd never seen a sight more beautiful. The Ford Plantation was a gorgeous place. For the sake of feigned propriety, John and Harriet followed a few paces behind us. The young fellow, William, was eager to show off all of his vast knowledge acquired from his travels. He told me about great wolves which are humans in disguise. But every month, when the moon is full, they turn and twist out of their human skin and become a great, powerful, hungry beast that devours humans without consciousness.

I remember thinking that while he probably embellished a lot of this, how different is that from how I kill? I tear and twist arms from a torso and drink blood. I rip out a throat and gorge myself on its owner. So I let him talk and tried to stir the conversation away from the wolf and towards creatures more like myself.
William nodded, deep in thought, and told me about vampires. He said they could turn into bats and wear long, dark capes. They collect virgins around themselves. I looked back at Harriet with a wink and remember her face darkening and her lips thinning in mock offense. The two of us had an easy time, a friendship even. I knew, of course, that Harriet was a virgin. But given this outrageous tale and the obvious need for me to apparently collect virgins, I wanted to make sure.
John silently chuckled to himself and we continued walking. I wonder what the bats were about. Can I turn into a bat? How would that work?
William kept trailing off every few paces, telling me about the softness of my hands, or the beautiful stars in my eyes and I kept thinking about how to turn into a bat. I closed my eyes hard and concentrated. William must have stopped and I stumbled into him. Very un-lady-like. I apologized profusely and put a dainty hand to my exposed throat in a sign of calculated embarrassment, just like Harriet suggested.
I asked him how the transformation would work. From vampire to bat, but William didn't have an answer. He told me vampires sleep in coffins and burn in the sun. Then he came closer and tried to look deep into my eyes and told me that he would protect me from the beasts with the large canines. I don't know why, but his gallantry made me smile widely, inadvertently exposing those just

149

mentioned large fangs. I laughed loudly and after a moment of shock, that was the end of poor William.

For almost a year we continued our travels. Through the West, the mountains, where the stories changed the rules of being a monster. But I never found one. I kept being told not to look for such darkness or eventually, it would come and find me. But if you already are the darkness, you need darkness to continue on.
Harriet and John became closer by the day and I saw their friendship blossom into love. I doubled their salary and told them that when the year is done, I'd leave them. Both protested, loving me and our adventure together. But I didn't want to continue burdening them, possibly killing one or both, breaking their hearts, or the rest of mine.
The last place we went to in our little trio was up north in the snow. Beautiful pine trees gave this place such a clean smell and the wind carried the sea salt all the way onto my skin. I loved it there.
Here we found the closest thing to another monster. We found truth. On one of the small islands, we bought board in a little inn. Comfortable and all made from wood. I sat with my two friends, ordering dinner from the in-keeper when the old man put down a glass of blood in front of me. We all got very, very quiet.
"Dinner is on the house, but I ask you to leave us and our island in peace, not in pieces." His voice was rough, darkened from decades of shouting and whiskey.
He stared at me, direct and unafraid. I touched the glass and pulled my hand back in shock. It was still warm.
"Goats blood. Not what you're used to, I'm afraid." He just held my gaze and I slowly rose to my feet. Keenly aware of him towering over me. Somehow this man intimidated me. I'm the deadly predator, but he made me fear him.
"I came here for answers. Not death." I heard myself tell him. I still had a girlish voice. Beautiful and full of melody.

"Whatever your kind comes for is of no matter. Death follows suit." His rough cadence was like the sea breeze. Fresh but un-inviting. He tried to turn but I took hold of his arm. I pulled back, gently returning his freedom, but I tried to ask one more time.

"Sir, we shall leave tonight. You have my word. But what do you know of my kind?" The man gave me half a glance and another to my two companions. Pity on his worn face.

"I know you won't die unless there is another." He said and to this day I don't know what he meant. He turned and left us. A barmaid came after, feeding my friends.

"You don't die unless there is another." Over the years those words return to me in frequent variations and tones. I wish he had told me more, but I respected him and his wishes.

I left before the end of the night, no goodbye for Harriet and John. Just a large sum of money and my necklace for my lovely, loyal friend. I wanted them to have a life.

For decades I came to visit the little village and seeing what happened to the two of them. They bought a little log shipping company and it grew every time I watched them from the shadows. I saw their children. First when they were little. Then years later, I came back and spotted the first signs of the passing time on Harriet. Her smooth skin had a few cracks from laughing. Beautiful, I thought. And John's pitch black, short-cropped curls had a few strands of silver in them. Made him look distinguished. I spoke to Harriet only one more time. She was a crone, surrounded by her children and grandchildren. It was winter. Just after Christmas. Snow covered their lovely property and lights danced in the window. She spotted me from the living room window and came out onto the back porch. Slowly, leaning heavily on a walking stick. We met in the snow as friends. The necklace I gave her in her youth and her wedding ring were the only jewelry gracing her body. I smiled at her and hugged her close.

"Did you get your answers?" She asked with a voice full of aches and small pains.

I petted her lovely hair and looked into her eyes.

"No, darling. Did you?" I asked, meaning all the beautiful fills of life she thought she'd never get to have when I met her on the steps of that brothel.

Her smile was wide and open and heart-braking.

"I have no more questions left." Her frail fingers squeezed my hands and I felt her love seeping into my body. What a gift she was to me. The both of them.

"You've lived the perfect life." I told her, ready to leave. I kissed each cheek and spotted tears in her eyes.

"Thanks to a demon and a great adventure." She smirked and her nose crinkled just like it used to.

"All the best adventures have a demon." I winked at her. She wasn't so willing to let me back into the night.

"We could go have another one?" A little of her youthful spark returned.

I looked through the window and saw a toddler, probably a grandchild or great-grandchild falling forward as they do, trying to walk their first steps. It made my smile lopsided.

"Your life is already full of them." I told her and nod towards the lights.

She turned and her hand touched her chest, appreciating every moment, good and bad.

When her eyes tried to find me again, they couldn't.

I think of her often. Even now. Every good adventure has a demon.

Yes. It sure does. Tonight, I'm just not sure whether the demon is me, or I'm about to meet one.

CHAPTER 29: THE FIGURE

For the first time in centuries, I have trouble keeping up. I follow the tall, lean man through the city. Alley by alley. Corner after corner. He knows this place intimately. It makes me wonder just how long he's been here waiting for me.

I can't get past that moment. In bed with Ness, holding her, consoling her. Just the two of us.

Then I felt it. A static within me. Buzzing. New. I knew instinctively what it was even though it was the first time. I could feel his approach and his hovering. Even the level of old, undiluted strength radiating off of him. This being is older than me.

I narrowly avoid the garbage can in my path as he rounds another bend. Where is he heading? I'm also starting to worry. I'm following something I have no idea about. What is he leading me into? But in moments of danger, I like to play a little game I call "worst case scenario". In this particular one, he'd probably kill me, which, if we're being honest, seems to be a hard thing to do, and if he succeeds, great. That's what I've been aiming for. What would he gain from my death?

I'm so curious that I almost don't see the car cutting off my pursuit. It almost hits me, horn blaring in annoyance and dirty puddle water splashing up my pants.

He glances over his shoulder and I swear I see a grotesque smirk. Not a pretty sight. He's tall and sculpted, meticulously dressed, albeit very outdated. His shirt is at least a few decades old, his pants reveal sock garters as he moves. His hair is bound together neatly by a small band at the base of the neck. An overcoat completes the ensemble. Half-long and most certainly hiding whatever weapons he favors most.

I managed to strap most of my knives and scalpels back to their various hiding places, but I was in a rush. I'm barefoot. Drawing attention from humans. Not wise. I'm without my jacket, which usually contains two sets of throwing knives and a curved, wicket short-sword strapped to the back. None of that is with me now. Instead, my long, light-blonde hair sways with every run and jump. I didn't even grab my hair band; rookie mistake. I must look insane to the passerby's and drivers. An older woman in her Fiat gives me a pitiful stare. Before she can finish rolling down her window to ask me whether I'm all right, I jump through the assembly of cars waiting for the light to turn green, and rush back into the darkness.

The alley is deserted. Only a rough-looking, murderously inclined cat calls it home. It meows at me with a foul-mouthed attitude of utter annoyance. I'm quite impressed. This small body can produce this much hate. "Me too, buddy." I answer its call for peace and look around me. I think I lost him. The figure is nowhere to be seen. I turn back to the street and the cars start the slow process of rolling through the intersection in their very human, orderly fashion.

Some light blurs into my spot and I try to feel where he went. The electric buzz remains within me. He must still be close. But I don't see him anywhere. My new feline friend hisses at me with pure dissent, wondering why on earth I haven't left his domicile. I lean down and give him a pat on his dirty head and he seems surprised for a second before he digs his small little fangs into my unbreakable skin. It makes me smile, he is sassy. Good for him. The little street lion comes up for air having realized it can't hurt me, and gives me one last glare before sauntering off, tail raised. I feel accepted.

The buzz inside grows and I know. I look up. Of course. I use the same trick. He stands even taller, two stories up, sneering down at me as though I was a peasant in front of his castle gates. There is no kindness in his old face. Sewn from granite. Perfect, not a wrinkle, but no love either. I'm not sure how the rules of my own existence work, but I think this creature was never human.

I jump and the ease of the movement feels freeing. One hand on the old windows of the boarded-up carriage house and one between the bricks. I have no trouble holding myself up. Old buildings also provide plenty of opportunities for climbing. The vines of ivy are strong and sturdy and help with another thrust upwards. Within seconds, I make it to the roof and half expect him to face me. But he's already gone again. I run across the flat surface and jump blindly, not fully knowing what's below. Mid-air I see more urban abandonment. Old factories, broken windows, wild and unattended greenery, and decades of loss of wealth and status.

Ponce City Market was once a bustling center full of economic hope for small traders and businesses. But when the train systems changed their route and the MARTA, or in its long form the Metropolitan Atlanta Rapid Transit Authority, avoided the area almost entirely, it lost access to a large consumer base and bled out faster than one of my victims. Now it's across from me. Empty and forlorn. Forgotten by the city for more lucrative endeavors. No one fixes buildings like this. Everyone just complains about poverty and homelessness, crime and despair, and moves on to the next topic.

I watch as my guide, the tall stranger, jumps faster than I ever have. With fluid ease, he lands on the upper perch, next to a broken window. He moves inside out of my view.

I gulp. It's a taunt. I know he wants me to follow him, but what am I walking into? His domain. He is no small cat that I can easily wrangle. He's very, very different. For a moment I stand still and let the wind play with my loose hair.

"Worst case scenario": I enter and die.

I feel out the words and somehow I don't like them. I have too many questions. I want to have them all answered first. He should kill me tomorrow.

Is it worth it? Following this being into the dark? But I'm already walking. Slowly.

I climb my second building of the night. This one offers much less hold. Its structure is unpleasant and brittle.

Half of my hand fills with dust at every turn. But I reach the window and ease myself into the unknown.

The air is different in here. A different kind of humid. It's quieter inside, blocking out the noise of the city.

Drip.

Oh no, my old friend, the dripping, taunting water has found me. It should send me running. I sneak forward, crouched down on one of the many exposed ceiling joists. They crisscross across the entire warehouse. Like an entire unused second floor, pillars and beams stretch across. Easy access. Eerie.

I hear a whimper. So frail and breakable. Human.

Instinctively my eyes check the exits. There is only one and it's locked. From what I have seen from my ancient counterpart, he'd outrun me to it.

Another whimper breaks my thoughts. What is that? I prowl a bit closer.

On the far side of the structure, I can see the tall man. He's approaching a set of large dog crates. No. Not dog crates. Not dog crates at all. Those are small cages for humans. It sucks the air out of me. I'm stunned. I kill. Sometimes I even enjoy it. I can't exactly call that moral high ground, but this is different. There are eight of them, waist high and unbreakable for human strength. Half stacked on top of the others.

About four or five of them are filled with terrified inhabitants. Their smell hits me like a brick. Urine, dirt, fear, and dried blood. The entire place stinks of it. The humidity soaks it up and it hangs and stays in the air with thick sweetness. If I had any human reactions, I would throw up.

Drip. My friend, the never-ending drip is also much less innocent than the last time. One of the caged victims is unconscious or dead. A young man, judging by his face, and he's unconscious and slowly bleeding onto the woman below him. Brutal.

The tall man unsheathes two twenty-inch blades from the back of his jacket with unnatural ease. So swift and fluid, I could learn a thing or two. He flips them through the air.

Undoubtedly for me. To impress. I'm sad to say that it works.

He has an unhurried and mesmerizing skill with the deadly weapons. Then he scratches the knives across the metal of the cages.

RATATATATAT.

Fast and Unnerving. The sound reverberates and echoes through the entire warehouse.

RATATATATAT.

I can feel it in my bones. It sets my teeth on edge. Like nails on a chalkboard, but drawn by someone who enjoys it. The pain.

A dirty, middle-aged man starts begging with a breaking voice.

"Please. Please let me go. I have a family. Here." His entire body shakes. His clothes are already torn and hang off his frail stature in rags. Out of the remainders of his pockets, he pulls an old, leather wallet. He's not a rich man. The leather is stained and shiny after much use. He unfolds it and lets a picture flop down. It's covered in a little plastic sheath.

"This is my daughter." He whines with more convulsions across his body. I can smell the different layers of his fear so clearly, it must be like ringing a dinner bell for the monster in front of him. This man is going to die today and not in a gentle way.

The dark figure stops in front of him. Cocking his head and looking at the tiny frame. I can't see what he sees from here. The plastic glares with reflecting light. But it seems as though my fellow immortal is, in fact, considering?

"I can pay you." The man continues. Hope flaring up in his voice, steadying a bit.

The figure lowers the wicked blades a bit. Does he have empathy? Maybe I was wrong. Maybe there is some humanity left in him.

157

I crawl a bit closer and the smell of blood turns my eyes silver. I can't control it, but I feel it happening. My hunting instinct snaps into place. Solid and reliable.

The dark figure points a long finger and traces it down the cage. His nail hitches slightly on the imperfections on the surface. He's like a cat. Toying with his kills. He palms the padlock on the front and gives it a gentle squeeze. It doesn't take much immortal strength for the small clasp to give in and burst into pieces. He uses the edge of his blade to unlatch the cage and the small door screeches as it slowly swings open.

This man is going to die. This freedom is fleeting. A trap. A game to his captor. I should help him. End him quickly and without pain, but somehow I can't move. I'm pinned to my spot, mesmerized and horrified in equal measure.

An inviting arm extends for the dirty man to exit. The long arms of the tall man seem much longer than they are, extended by the deadly blades.

Hesitation. Fear. Undiluted, pungent fear. But the human slowly crawls out of his cage. He stumbles and almost falls on a bending knee. He must have been a captive for some time, not using his legs. A groan of pain escapes him and his legs shake from strained muscles.

"Thank you. I promise I won't say anything. Ever. Thank you so much." His voice breaks weakly.

You sure won't say a thing, I think to myself. This man is going to die.

Knees weak he tumbles a few steps. The dark figure slowly turns to face him. His old immortal eyes shine silver, like mine. I gulp and shrink a little into myself. He's terrifying.

With a screech, high-pitched and bone-shattering, exposing his fangs and true intentions, the dark figure sends the dirty man into a stumbling run with only one possible destination.

My own hands shiver. I should end this cruel display of brutality. But somehow I cannot. I'm glued to my spot.

For the very first time, I hear the dark figure speak. It's somehow less pleasant than his appearance. A rasping sound.

He counts. A ticking clock for his victim to know exactly just how many seconds of life remain.

"Five. Four."

The blades twirl through the air again, elegant and light. He tosses them into the air, takes off his overcoat, and catches both behind his back. What a show-off.

The dirty man beelines for the door. His legs falter but he reaches it. A hint of relief on his haggard face. But it's locked. He shakes it to the best of his weaning strength. It doesn't budge.

"Three. Two." The figure's voice carries. Up to me in the rafters and certainly down to his petrified victim. The man rattles the lock. But it won't give for him.

The dirty man looks behind him into the darkness. He cannot see where the dark figure has gone and aimlessly stumbles behind the next pillar. From my perfect, high vantage point I see this cat and mouse game unfold in all of its sad glory.

"One." I hear the countdown finish and the warehouse is shrouded in eerie silence.

Only two small sounds disrupt it. The drip of the unconscious body and the man's fast-paced heartbeat. It beats so quickly, that it seems to want to break out of his chest. With a little help, it just might.

The quiet is unnerving. The dirty man peers around the pillar to spot the impending danger but to no avail. I too have lost sight of the figure. He's an immaculate hunter. Much better than me.

The dirty man tries to hide the noise in every breath that escapes him. Squinting into the darkness.

A clinking noise from far behind catches his attention. The bouncing of metal. The dirty man shivers with fear. There, across the room. A light. The back door is slightly ajar. What a tease, I think to myself. Giving hope.

159

But before he can truly steady himself, another SCREECH, inches from his face. Silver eyes glaring with hunger. Close and vicious.

The dirty, broken man runs. Limping deeply. Heaving breaths unable to truly fill his lungs with much strength. This is sad. It's callous and not at all the way I kill.

He squints in pain and continues to hurry forward. So close. The light expands in front of him. He reaches out for the door handle. So close. His fingers almost touch it, just as -

A high-pitched whizzing sound breaks the thick air and stops everything cold.

Feet wiped out from under him, a pulley system, similar to an old animal trap, pulls the dirty man up. He hangs upside down, whimpering loudly.

His fear is palpable as he wets himself, body shaking from its center. He never stood a chance. But to give him hope. What a barbarous thing to do.

Assured footsteps approach with casual ease. Like a pleasant Sunday morning.

"Please." The human begs again. But even he knows it won't bear fruit.

Face to face with death. The dirty man stares into those shiny, silver eyes. Expert speed and precision accompany the two blades, as the dark figure stabs deep and slices down the dirty man's wrists lengthwise.

The dark figure groans in malevolent pleasure. Savoring the smell of blood. This game is his life.

One last WHIMPER, then the blades fly again, down the length of both sides of the man's neck. Blood gushes out like a flowing river, fast and steady.

With a blink, the dark figure indulges and lets the blood warm his outstretched tongue.

There is a sensuality to it that makes me feel entirely uneasy. I stalk closer, teeth bare with the hunger blood naturally brings to me. I can't help it. I watch the body of the dirty man jerk in the throws of clinging to life. The

160

movement becomes smaller, a twitch and it continues to ebb.

The dark figure plunges his teeth deep into the exposed throat. Gorging himself. Gulping with thick bursts of pleasure.

Almost passionately, his hand glides up the jerking body's chest, to his soft belly, digging his nails into flesh. The skin rips and specks of blood turn into small streams as the dark figure's grip turns forceful and claws down. This is sexual to him. The act of hunting, feeding, and becoming, I realize and the thought disgusts me.

He pauses and steps back. Blood dripping from his chin.

"Time to come out now, little darling. I may even let you have a taste first." His voice has a melody to it, strange and old.

With freezing horror, I realize he's speaking to me.

As he licks his fingers clean, his silver eyes turn slowly but focused to lock on my own.

CHAPTER 30: OPEN EYES

His eyes make my stomach drop with, what is this feeling? Fear? I remember it vaguely from centuries ago. I last felt it the night my family died and I was turned into the creature I am now. It crawls from the inside of my neck all the way down to the pit of my stomach. It tingles. Not pleasantly and without control.

I watch him slowly licking his fingers clean with a small moan. I shudder in disgust. He enjoys riling me up and a sadistic smile bends his mouth to one side. With one smooth, feline jump, he lands across me on the ceiling beam. He's much faster than me and he knows it. Like a predator scaring a rival into submission, he calmly rises to his full, impressive height in front of me. I force myself to stand tall myself, hiding my fear.

He inhales like a sommelier would a marvelous wine. I realize, he's judging my scent. But for what? Is he going to do what he did to the man below us? Cut me to ribbons and drink me dry? He can't. I cannot die. He couldn't kill me.

"Bold of you to come visit me."

His voice isn't a welcome sound. It is underused, raspy, and full of threat. An itch under my skin that won't go away.

"I am so much stronger and older than you. Why risk it?" As he speaks, he wipes his dirty blades on his pants, staining them with his victim's blood. I watch him with horrid fascination, realizing he asked me a question. Confusion spreads through me. Risk what?

"I'm like you. I cannot die." I tell him and hear my own voice sounding like the one of a child.

The dark figure grins. Stained teeth. Not a pretty sight. He cocks his head and twirls one of his shiny blades through the blood-humid air.

"Of course, you can. I'll teach you."

For a split second his words ring through me. Comprehension is slow to follow. But then they hit me like a ton of bricks, stunning me for too long to see what dire situation I've put myself into.

He lunges. A slice of the right blade misses me by hair's breadth as I instinctively let myself drop down a level. I land on my feet but they slide in the dead man's blood. I am hopelessly outmatched.

The monster follows, feinting with the left sword, but stabbing with the right. Only centuries of experience and my father's lovely scalpels give me a fighting chance.

I duck and the attack misses again. With a flick of my wrists, my gauntlets release their own blades, thinner and much sharper than his, and I slice with precision. My father's surgical tenacity taught me that well-curated specificity can save a life. Let's hope he's right.

My curved blade finds purchase and slices through the dark figure's pants. Not deeply, but enough to make him withdraw his vicious attack and move backward. He underestimated me. But I have made the same mistake with him and I've already come to regret it. I let myself fall backward and roll. The more space between me and him, the better. I land on my naked feet. My knees are bent and nimble and I bounce from one leg to the other, watching my opponent with alertness.

No one taught me to fight. There was never truly a need for it. I've always been the alpha anywhere I went. But I did learn a few things to kill quicker and impose less trauma and pain on my victims.

He grins at me and his hideous smile splits his face in two. Then he screeches, shrill and petrifying. It startles me and I lose my focus.

He uses the temporary distraction and jumps up. Out of sight.

I try desperately to trace him but his footsteps are silent, even for my preternatural auditory ability. My eyes dart across every inch, every beam across. He could be anywhere. He could jump down from behind me and slice without warning.

With his swords, he will be better equipped to be further away when inflicting damage. My scalpels are deadly, but I need to come very, very close. Too close for comfort. I have the wrong weapons for this. I brought a knife to a gunfight. Then I hear his voice again. It bounces off the walls.

"I can smell who died to make you, little birdie." His words echo across the vaulted ceiling, making it impossible to pinpoint their origin.

Died to make me? I don't have time to think about the meaning. But I don't need to. He continues explaining.

"Daddy left you very vulnerable by not explaining the rules to you."

Cold dread runs through every inch of me. Daddy. He knows that my father made me. How? Rules? He knows how to die and probably knows how to create. I steady myself. Maybe I can get the answers I need from him? Maybe it would buy me some time with Ness?

"He only did it to save me." I yell into the darkness. My eyes gleam with silver fire. C'mon. Where are you?

"And did he? Saaaaave you?" He croons with a lover's purr and it makes my skin crawl. I shiver all the way down to my toes. The voice is behind me and I spin, careful not to slide in the drying blood covering the floor. I'm on my toes, ready. To attack or defend, I'm uncertain. There, a shadow?

"Oh, the good doctor. Clever little brother."

The words stop me cold. Little brother? That would make this creature I'm fighting, my uncle.

"My father was your brother?" All I earn is a laugh from the echo.

"Yes. My beloved, little brother. We grew up together, survived capture together until..."

I want to hear him speak about my father, tell me everything he knows.

"Until what? What do you know?" I can hear my own impatience and it makes me sound so very young. He's toying with me and I've just given him a new way to do it.

"You never wondered about his name?" He asks me as more confusion spreads across my face. From wherever he is hiding, he must be able to read it because he continues.

"Tepeš Lucârd."

Before I can think and search my own mind for any clues, the monster lands behind me and I whirl, face to face with his smirking grimace. He's enjoying this. I'm feeding right into his game, whatever that might be.

"Tepeš is a Romanian word. Very old. It means to spike, or to impale."

My jaw slackens as the realization creeps in. No. That can't be right. The books were wrong. Nothing was ever truthful or even remotely right about this.

"But his last name..." I blurt out the half question, but I don't think I really need him to answer. He does anyway, giving his natural, Slavic drawl free rein. His voice didn't actually have a rasp, he was just trying to cover his accent.

"Say it backward." He almost sneers.

No. No, no, no. Not my father. It's nothing more than a fantasy tale. But I can't help myself and oblige.

"Lucârd - Dracul"

There it is. A truth I didn't figure out for centuries. I think about Bram Stoker and his book. He was wrong. His story was fiction. But I remember reading about the history of Vlad the Impaler. A prince in his own right, who as a child was a captive in the Ottoman empire, now Turkey. There, he and his brother were tortured and watched torture happen to others. This knowledge he later applied in his battles and impaled his victims on spikes on the battlefield, earning himself the name, Vlad the Impaler. I remember reading about him being part of an old organization called the Order of the Dragon, which gave him the second part of his name; Dracul.

Brother. The word doesn't leave my mind and pulses through me like a sickly heartbeat. Which brother am I standing in front of? Which one was my father? Which

166

secret was worse for my father to keep? Who his brother was? Or what he did hundreds of years ago in battles across Europe? This can't be right. This can't be real. Yet, I know what I am. I know I thrive on blood and thirst and killing myself. Before I have time to ponder the details of my existence again, the monster lunges.

I'm caught off guard and one of his blades pierces through my shoulder with ease and no opposition from my own scalpels. He spikes me to the pillar behind me.
A deep inhale and I feel my pupils widen. Like a dull, rusted screw through my spine, from the nape of my neck to the bottom of my heel, the pain of the wound stings through my body. He actually hurt me. I'm not healing. My eyes go in and out of their blue and silver transition. Pain. Searing and numbing. Pain. He pinned my shoulder, scratched the clavicle from below, and skewered through the scapula, the blade bone in the back. I haven't felt this in centuries and forgotten what this is like. A scream escapes me, delayed and breathless. A surprise. He can injure me. I think he's going to be able to kill me too.
He brings his blood-drenched, crusted lips close to my ear. I can feel his smile build. I can't pull away.
"The Order of the Dragon was a family. A very large family with wide connections across nobility and clergy."
I have trouble hearing him right. The pain continues. He ever so slowly leans down on his blade, the weight of it digging further into me. Then he licks down my face. A gesture of ownership and dominance. His foul breath is wretched.
His eyes glaze over with lust as he looks at my shoulder wound. He bends down and licks off a bit of my blood too.
I realize I'm bleeding. Freely. He follows my train of thought.
"Oh, you can die, darling. But only another immortal can kill you." I finally have an answer to one of my most important questions. The clarity doesn't outweigh the

pain. Ness comes across my mind. Her beautiful, soft skin. I wonder if she'll stop looking for me. Will she go back to her perfect life? I should have never interfered with her world and left her alone.

"Then kill me. End it."

My voice is steady and full of determination. I'm grateful it doesn't reflect my inner turmoil. Is this still all I want? Die? A few wonderful years with Ness sound exhilarating. There are answers about my family. There are others out there. I am not alone. But it's too late.

He laughs and traces his blood-smeared, filthy hands sensually down my thin-layered shirt.

He enjoys every squirm as he touches and explores me; every curve, my rage only fueling his pleasure. I snarl at him. Feral and ready to rip his throat out of his body. His chuckle is like an icy hail storm, unforgiving.

"I'd rather see how much of your father is in you first. We were very close once. He and I. Until he abandoned us all."

He presses himself against me, licking down my neck and I can feel the male excitement rising to his brutal, sadistic actions. It makes me sick and I scream trying to move against the blade. New pain shoots through me as the wound widens. It almost numbs my senses.

"There is this other, sweet scent all over you."

A vile moan escapes his dirty mouth and I try to kick him where it matters, but he's too quick. He grabs me and cradles my hips with a sense of ownership, spreading my knees with his and moving me against himself. I want to tear him apart limb by limb. He can injure me. Kill me if he must. I've killed plenty myself. But he doesn't get to smell Ness on me, think about her or -

"I think I fancy a midnight stroll."

He chimes and moves off of me. I try to hold onto him but he's gone faster than my eyes can follow. Now my pain is followed by something much worse. Fear. Undiluted and all-consuming. He's going to kill her.

CHAPTER 31: VISITORS - LUKE

The mood is somber. After the whale shark tank had been cleaned, management proceeded to call in each employee individually and ask them a series of accusatory questions. The culprit has yet to be found. No one knows who threw blood into the aquarium's crown jewel and caused the feeding frenzy. But all agreed that it was more than just a prank. It must have taken a considerable amount of strength and coordination to lift the feeding lid and dump a large enough volume of gore into it to make seeing the fish impossible from the viewing deck.

No one saw anything and the security footage came back empty. George and his team, a tight-knit, experienced security company, got very worried that they missed something and would be let go. But there was nothing to miss.

Management asked me too, the moment I got in. We went over every inch of my laboratory, every employee, and every entry protocol.

That's when we started double-checking the entryways. George remembered that two years ago, some delivery drivers tried and failed to break in and steal a dolphin. He told us that because of budget cuts they didn't add a camera, but simply angled the one from the trash door close by. He added that the trainers sometimes still sneak out there and make good use of that fact, by taking more than their allotted smoking breaks and leaving the door unlocked.

Management immediately sought to remedy the situation and now, I'm standing next to a very concerned George, who shows me the latest security footage of a break-in.

I can hardly believe my eyes. I'm looking at my own girlfriend. I watch as he presses the playback button one more time. Hood drawn too tightly around her face, Ness checks left and right before sneaking in between the two large trash compactors in the loading dock. Then, with a surprising lack of subtlety, she looks straight into the lens of the security camera above the door, likely thinking it's still turned the other way. With a satisfied grin, she removes the paper propping open the door and slips inside.

Both George and I know that Ness would never mess with the whale shark tank. She's also physically not capable of dropping tons of bloody feed in. But why is she breaking into the aquarium? Why didn't she call me? I'm glad I stayed longer than my schedule dictates, so I can fix this. I just don't understand it. She knows I shouldn't be here right now. So why come in?

George shows me her whereabouts on the camera. She's in my lab. I'm stupefied for a moment watching her watch Socrates, my test subject and then rummage through my papers. I'm just stunned. Ness has little interest in my research. She sometimes pokes fun at it, but she would never sabotage me. What is she doing? This doesn't seem like her at all.

I can't even move into action, I'm so beside myself with shock.

"Do you want me to talk to her?" George asks me with the gentleness of someone knowing this won't end well.

I shake my head slowly. This is not who my girlfriend, my future fiancé is.

"I'm sure something serious happened. She would never..." But even George trails off, lacking explanations. Something has been happening. Ness changed. The last few days have been very different. I felt it last night too. Making love to her was like begging for her attention and her heart. Both things she usually gives so willingly and with playful love. I hardly recognize the person on the screen. Frantic and disheveled. Desperate and with deep shadows beneath her eyes. She looks like she hasn't slept for a week.

"I'll take care of it." I tell George, but my voice sounds heavy with sadness.

I turn to him but he already winks at me with a crooked smile.

"I won't tell management." I nod my thanks. I know it wasn't her with the blood in the tank, but this doesn't

170

look good for her or me. She's risking my position without a second thought. That selfishness is something I've never seen in her. My heart races, anxiety and shock still battling within. I'm not sure which one will win out. I'm so incredibly disappointed. What could Ness possibly want with my research?

I speed through the halls of the aquarium and not even the deep blue calms me down. Everything feels claustrophobic and heavy.

The elevator is stuck. On top of everything. So I take the stairs. Metal and loud with each step down. I reach the lab door and watch for a moment through the glass. She's just reading.

A distant crash sounds somewhere and it would take my full attention, except Ness' eyes land on my own and I enter.

I can't believe how well that worked. The aquarium is such a fortress. I feel very accomplished remembering the little details about the cameras and the secret smokers. The tunnels are dark and only lit via LED strips at ankle height. It gives the whole place an ominous glow. Above me, the whale sharks sleep. Or whatever it is that they do at night. I'm not a hundred percent certain they sleep. They probably calmly float about regardless of their waking or non-waking state. Adrenaline pumps through me with steady fervor. I just broke into a place. A place I know well, but still. I, the girl who used to strive for perfection and adored rules, even wrote them for others to follow, broke into a place and committed a serious crime.

I huff a laugh at myself and round the corner to the elevator. The doors are wide open but it's out of service. So strange. A flash of memory creeps through my mind. Spindly long fingers held the door open for me with strange, cold elegance. The THING that Grace is following was here. I'm sure of it now. I wasn't seeing things or making things up. He was real. Very, very real. I turn to take the stairs and glance into the main hallway with trepidation. No one has come looking for me. Likely, George is alone on his shift searching YouTube for the cutest cat video. Bless his heart.

The thought makes me feel safe enough to untie the knot I fastened of the hood I fastened under my chin. I meant a little too well and its tightness of it gave my face very little freedom. I shake my hair out as I lower the restrictive fabric and take a deep breath. The curls spring free and I take the metal stairs down.

The lab glows up for me. I know Luke never wanted cameras in here unless there was an emergency with the aquarium, so I feel safe. I managed to break in and reach my destination. The tanks are all lit from below and the creatures in them remind me of the slow-moving lava lamps everyone had in the early 2000s. I smile at the thought and wonder if the immortal jellyfish in front of me would be offended by the comparison.

Socrates bulbs up as if in greeting. Charmingly strange. He sparkles up with electricity and I wonder whether it is in recognition, to fight, or to devour me whole. With Luke's sea-creatures it doesn't just have to be one of the three. I place my hand on the glass and watch his immortal grace float about.

"Hey buddy, so how do you do it? What's your secret?" I must have officially lost my remaining marbles. I'm speaking to a jellyfish. I just really hope he doesn't actually answer, otherwise I will know for certain that I have indeed lost it.

But Socrates just gives me a little show and twirls his gangly body through the small currents in the tank. I watch him play with the air bubbles from the filter. He's almost cute. Deadly, immortal, and adorable. One of his tentacles reaches out for my hand. Aww, he shares my sentiment. He sparks up brighter.

A small jolt of pain shoots through my hand and I withdraw in surprise. His electricity burned me through the glass once again. For a split second, I ponder the possibility of it being imagined, but the sting in my hand is very real. My eyebrows bunch together and I stare at my immortal frenemy.

"Well, you too then." I tell him and move away from his tank. Maybe he's not as cute as I first thought.

I walk past and stare at the wall boards. Next to them are tubes and jars that fill the various desks. Contemplating. I squint and try to figure out what part of the gibberish in front of me can tell me about eternal life. Why does it have to be chemical formulas and math? I sigh. This is not what I was hoping for.

The shelf containing the specimen samples might be more helpful. I start reading the labels.

'Soc_12/09/22_batch5_urine'

I almost drop it reading the last word. I'm holding jellyfish pee. I shake my head at myself. Maybe the secret is really in the -
No, no it isn't. I refuse to believe that's what will give me the chance to be with Grace forever. I will not attempt to drink this.
The next vial gives me pause.

'Soc_11/26/22_batch5_blood_promising***'

It has three stars. On Yelp that could get you quite far if you know how to play your cards right. Do I risk it? The key has to be somewhere in the blood. It just makes sense. Right?
I unscrew the top and stare at the light blue fluid. It smells absolutely horrid. My nose crinkles and I frown. This little beast does not smell good in any shape or form. I steady myself. Let's just do it. I pinch my nose shut and raise the vile to my lips.
One more exhale and here we go. Bottoms up. I gulp and gag. This is hard to keep down. I wave my hand in front of my mouth like I'm putting out a fire when I hear a crash somewhere above me. I look around and find none other than Luke staring back at me through the glass door. Fuck.

CHAPTER 33: HELP IN DARK PLACES - GRACE

The pain, this unknown feeling is mind-numbing. I cannot say that I've missed this. Blood is seeping through my thin undershirt and slowly covering me all the way down to my waist. I can feel my eyes changing back and forth from blue to silver. My flawless, lethal body is as confused as I am. But I need to go. I need to find Ness and keep her safe. He's going to kill her in her bed. Her mother too. If she had the good sense to go to work, then he'll kill her mother and then follow Ness' scent all the way through the city. Like I did when I first saw her.

The thought makes me angry and fills me with panic. I take a deep breath and hold the air in as I try to strain against the blade still stuck through my shoulder, deep into the wall behind me. I scream so loudly that I'm sure I can be heard miles away. Usually, I would care, but not today.

Close behind me, I hear a throat clearing in one of the cages. A woman is trying to get my attention.

"I'll help you, just let me out."

She rasps and I am surprised at her steadiness. She just watched another prisoner get torn apart brutally, then watched two immortals go for each other's throats but she has the guts to pipe up regardless and offer me help?

"I can't move." I reply, unable to look her in the face.

"I'm right next to you." She pipes and I slowly try to twist my head. Her small hands extend slightly through the crate.

I'm sure her offer is not entirely selfless. If I let her free, who's to say she won't just run away and leave me here to rot? That's what I would do in her situation. That's what she should do.

But she currently is my only option to get to Ness in time and try to hold off this monstrous uncle of mine. Uncle. This thing is related to me. I push the thoughts out of my head and focus on the immediate need.

"I'm a doctor, I'll patch you up." The lady continues. Normally I would laugh, but even the small huff escaping my mouth hurts so much that it almost causes me to faint. I manage to glare at her out of the corner of my eye. Nothing to lose. She runs, she runs. If she frees me, we've saved two lives. With my free hand, I reach out. Tapping the lock, but I'm not able to really grab hold of it. Another labored groan of pain escapes me. I feel the weakness spreading through me like a cancer.

I pull against the knife. More blood streams out of the gaping wound but I manage to palm the lock. Squeezing it with all my remaining strength. A few heavy breaths fill the pauses between. Another squeeze. It pops open. Finally. I am amazed at the difference between the monster and myself. He is so much stronger. It didn't take much for him to break the same lock.

The dirty woman climbs out of her confinement. She steps around me, whether to sneer at me and run away or to burn my face into her mind to tell authorities, I cannot say.

But she does neither and stays true to her word. Without so much as a look into my eyes, she examines the wound with swift, practiced hands.

"We're going to have to pull the blade out together. This is going to hurt." She tells me with the detached efficiency of a trauma surgeon. I can only blink at her.

"Why aren't you running?" I find myself asking her.

Her eyes find mine. No compassion or hate, just simplicity.

"I swore a Hippocratic Oath." She replies and I admire her true and stern integrity. I wish there were more people like her. Then her scent hits me fully and my eyes turn silver. In between the grime and the few days of imprisonment, I smell it clear as day, blood. I struggle against the urge and our hands meet at the blade as she starts finding leverage to help me pull it out.

"You have to go. You're bleeding." I order her. But she does no such thing.

"That time of the month. I can't control it." She says and checks the angle of the blade. She disregards my order and I try to growl to scare her off, but she starts her doctor countdown without any further discussion.

"On three."

"Please run. Now." I beg her, knowing that when I'm weak, I will kill even if I don't mean to. My eyes stopped changing back to blue. I can almost taste her.

Our hands interlock with strength.

"One, two..." And like any good doctor, she pulls on two, not three, so that there is no flinching and the expectation of pain is replaced by surprise and quick relief. I SCREAM. It's bone-chilling even for me to hear it. But the blade moves and as the woman stumbles back with the force of the movement, the sword clatters to the ground. A deep inhale centers me within my body. I have my freedom back. The last clink of the metal coincides with my teeth piercing the doctor's neck. Deep into her throat. I can't control it and drink deeply. Bursts of life coming back to me. I feel ashamed as I gulp. Horrible and like the true demon that I am.

I don't make her suffer and with a quick twist, I break her slender neck, putting her out of her misery. Her body collapses into my arms and I ease her gently onto the floor.

"I'm so sorry." I tell her and mean it.

My stomach is still convulsing with the gagging reflex when Luke enters. I've never once seen his face this livid. Like a storm cloud. I gulp, feeling shameful. I gag again but manage to keep down the jellyfish blood. There is no good way to explain this to him. I can't talk myself out of this situation. He also truly deserves some honesty.

"You really are crazy." He states, fighting to keep his voice calm, but I can hear his anger. He's furious.

"That was all we could extract and you have no idea what it could do to you." The cold realization hits me with his words. This could very well kill me, not grant me coveted immortality. I also just took part of his research, the work he fought so hard for, and destroyed it. I feel rotten to the core. All I thought about was Grace. Luke barely even crossed my mind. This beautiful, kind-hearted man standing in front of me deserves more than that. I sigh. I can't even tell him just how sorry I am. It wouldn't suffice.

"Well, now you'll at least see if it'll work." I try to joke but even to me it sounds stupid. Making light of what I have just done isn't a good tactic. It also clearly doesn't work on him. His jaw drops in utter disbelief. I've rendered him speechless. Somehow that doesn't stop my words from continuing on their treacherous path of destruction.

"C'mon, you wanted to drink it yourself too." I joke again and a few days ago I would not only never have said that, but I would also have wanted to slap myself for the irresponsibility, the selfish thoughtlessness, and callous behavior. But this is not the me from a few days ago. This is love-drunk Ness who fell for a melancholic vampire and wants to give her a reason to stick around.

Luke rummages around under his desk and produces a spit-bucket. He shoves it in my direction.

"I'm not playing around here. You can't break into my lab and drink anything you find. This is dangerous."

I hear so many emotions in his voice that it would break my heart if it wasn't already otherwise occupied. I turn the vial in my hand and read the label out loud.

"Soc_11/26/22_batch5_blood_promising***" He shoves the bucket closer as I twist the label and read the hastily scribbled notes on the back.

"'Socrates/Immortality?/Holy Grail.' I'm not drinking anything I find. I wanted to put your theory to the test."

I burp. Eternity doesn't become me. It also tastes like shit. Luke shakes his head. Disappointment and pain in his expression. So palpable I can almost touch it.

"Who is he?" He asks and I'm stunned. He knows that I've cheated. That I'm not his anymore. He's only a little bit wrong in his question. What do I say? What can I say? "I already told you -" I start, but he interrupts me and I'm glad he does.

"Then why do you have a hickey on your neck?"

In a moment of dread, I touch my flawless skin. Instinct. Luke retracts, moving further away from me. His face falls flat. Certainty. Now he knows it's true. I didn't even give him the courtesy of being honest. I know he played me with the question but I'm the one we're both ashamed at.

"I don't even know what's worse. You running off with some guy, or you not even having enough respect for me not to lie to my face." His voice breaks and I drop my hand from my neck. I try to explain.

"It's not what you think. It's very complicated."

His shallow nod is hard to watch. I've irreversibly broken something in him and between us. No going back. The perfect life is gone. He turns, ready to leave but sways on the spot, waiting for something. I won't ask him to stay. I won't give him any false hope either. But then it occurs to me that I am the one in his space, not the other way around. I was the one breaking into his place of work and messing with his research. Heat rises to my cheeks and I look at my feet. I put the small, empty vial on the table and ready myself to leave when I hear it. Clear as day. Luke does too.

Steps click in the hallway. Calm and calculated. Not hurried but determined. Luke's head whirls to me with anger.

"Did you bring him here?" His voice is full of accusations. How could I!?

But I shake my head in confusion.

"There is no guy." I tell him but he scoffs at me. Hurt flashing across his perfect features.

"Did you call security on me?" I ask, even though I have no right to ask for his leniency.

"No." He blurts out as though that would be a ridiculous idea. Another thought occurs to me as we both listen to the steps approach closer and closer.

"Grace?" I squint into the dim light as a shadow blocks out the glass in the entry door.

Luke just stares at me as he understands fully what that means. Yes, I nod at him. His suspicion is half true. I cheated on him. But not with another man. I can see him scanning my face for the person he loved, gone now. Maybe she never really existed and was just an idea of how I wanted to be.

But we don't have time for existentialism as the steps halt entirely and a knife blade SCREECHES along the glass. Now I know who the person on the other side of the door is. It's not Grace. The gravity of the situation sinks in.

Another screech splits the air and both Luke and I cover our ears as best as we can.

"What is that?" He asks in shock and disbelief.

I know what IT is but it would take far too many words to explain it to him and this is literally the worst moment to ask him to trust me.

The lights die out with one last sputtering flicker. Pitch black darkness surrounds us. I grab Luke's hand and he squeezes back. I'm so grateful that I would love to hug him and never let him go. The glass tables' lights come back to life, courtesy of the backup generator doing its best in case of emergencies. My eyes adjust and what I see makes my skin prickle with ice-cold fear. The door

183

sways back and forth. We're not alone in here anymore. Luke follows my gaze and train of thought.

We back up a few steps against the tank behind us. Both of us are staring into the dark trying to pinpoint an intruder.

Something shiny twists through the air, barely missing my ear. I feel the breeze on my neck. Then the fish tank behind us BURSTS INTO A THOUSAND PIECES with a crash.

Drenched in water and shock, we spin to look. Nothing. Just bits of coral wash up at my feet.

"Run." I breath to him. I know what's toying with us and I know we stand very little chance of survival. Luckily I don't have to convince Luke. He pulls me towards the staircase, my hand securely interlinked with his. It makes my heart feel a little lighter.

Another tank SHATTERS behind us. I turn my head. Socrates spills on the ground. Flailing and not able to cling to his immortality. His sassy electricity is gone. No color. Just grey and lifeless as a shoe spreads his body into the tiled floor without mercy.

I look up at the culprit and meet a pair of glinting, silver eyes. They are like Grace's, beautiful and mesmerizing, but this man's eyes are different. They have an ancient cruelty in them. My heart sinks within my chest. If he's here, that means that Grace is...I can't finish the thought. I don't want to finish the thought.

Luckily I have no time to. Luke pulls me into the stairwell.

We sprint up, not daring to glance behind us. Luke yanks at the first door and we squeeze through. He punches the glass of the emergency fire case hard and frees the fire extinguisher inside. I watch him use it to bar the door. He simply rams the lever just below the handle, so it's impossible to push down. Smart, albeit his now bruised hand. He shakes it out a bit, with no time for further examinations. But before I have time to be impressed with his ingenuity, we continue to run through the tunnels of the dark aquarium. The backup generator is only set to give energy to the most valuable assets, that being the fish and their filter pumps. So, the only light in here comes from the eerie water tanks.

We round another corner and find ourselves in the Preserved Exhibit, usually one of my favorites, but it's genuinely terrifying when only lit by a few aquariums on the side. The shadows are large and ominous. Skeletons of sharks and a menagerie of other sea creatures surround us frozen in time. They seem to loom above us, reaching out with monstrous grasps.

We slow a bit and he releases my hand. Our wet hair clings to both of our faces and confusion and fear are palpable.

"We need to run, he'll keep coming." I tell Luke, trying to sound as factual as possible, but it's challenging.

His face bunches up in question and worry. What do I know, he seems to ask breathlessly.

But before I can answer, I hear a door crash open.

Luke's face pales. It's the one he securely shut with the fire extinguisher.

"That's impossible. You'd need tons and tons of physical pressure per square inch to open that-" He stops himself from continuing and stares at me. I look down sheepishly. How do I explain what I know? I can't. He wouldn't believe me and it would take so many carefully considered words to make him understand. Before I can figure any of them out and try, he screams. A bone-curdling sound that has me by his side with immediate urgency.

A sharp bone, likely from this very exhibit, impales his right calf muscle. It pokes out the other side of his leg, covered in his blood.

"Fuck." He heaves out, pain straining his voice.

The creature must be close. Close enough to see us clearly, even if we cannot. We both know it.

Then I see it. Two silver dots in the darkness. Approaching with slow determination. Is that a snicker I hear?

"Take it out." Luke rasps, trying to see if he can put weight on his injured leg. His ankle works. Good.

Another bone breaks somewhere, unseen by us, and it's hurdled towards us. I twist Luke and myself to the side and the bone hits the wall, sticking out of the soft wall cover like a butter knife in the sun. I lock eyes with Luke and take a hold of the bone in his flesh. He squeezes my hand, knowing this will hurt and I yank, once, hard. He yelps as the shard comes free, blood gushing from his leg. But we're free to limp forward as best as we can manage. I maneuver myself under his shoulder and take a bit of his weight to help pull him through the hallway. Behind us, I do indeed hear a snicker.

CHAPTER 35: THE BIGGER MONSTER - GRACE

I should mourn the death of the wonderful human who just freed me. She deserves nothing less. But I don't have the time. After her, I decided to release the other remaining prisoners from their earthly hell as well. Likely not the way they would have enjoyed, but they knew too much. This was really more of a kindness. Like putting a hurt animal out of its misery.

I run so hard that my legs burn. I don't recognize the sensation at first but as I stumble, I think that this must be what humans mean when they speak about fatigue. I don't particularly like it. It slows me down.

I jump up Ness' roof and cold dread fills my chest. I can't smell her scent. But before I can catch her on the wind through the city, her bedroom window opens and a gently-faced, older woman stares at me in question. Her mother.

"I think introductions are in order." She says and smiles at me, as I still crouch on her roof.

It takes me by surprise.

"Well, c'mon in." She chirps at me. This is a terrible time for this, but I shouldn't refuse her either. I enter through the little window and close it behind me, following her through the bedroom, the hallway, to the downstairs of the pretty Brownstone.

"Next time, be a dear and use the front door, won't you? Better than leaving footprints on the new shingles. We just had the roof redone last year." Her voice is jovial and friendly. I'm so surprised by it. I catch a glimpse of myself in the mirror, covered in gore and blood. But before I can say a single word, she tosses me a hoodie. She's so maternal. I put it on and follow her into the kitchen. At least my face is miraculously clean from residue. A small mercy, I think.

In the kitchen, she pours two cups of coffee, one for me I realize. Oh, I'll have to pretend to drink this. She hands me the steaming liquid. Coffee. My hands shake and I smell it with caution, hiding my gag reflex, but not very well.

"Ah, ok. No need for it then." She says matter-of-factly and takes the cup from me. I realize something entirely mind-boggling. She's not afraid of me.

"Ma'am, I would love to talk to you for as long as you like, but I have to find Ness." She eyes me, still barefoot, I realize.

"Your shoes are in the corner, I took the liberty of drying them. They were soaked through." I follow her gaze and find my shoes under the space heater in the hallway. I take them and slip inside, tying them neatly. Next to them is my short sword laid out on a towel and cleaned professionally.

"No worries, I cleaned it like I clean my scalpels." She says as if this was nothing out of the ordinary for her.

"You are clearly in a hurry, I won't hold you long, but if you're going to be spending time with my daughter, I thought at least, I'd like to know your name and ask you to stop using the upper...entrance." Fair enough. I already admire her. Strong, no-nonsense, and straightforward. A woman after my own heart.

"My name is Grace, Graciella, but Grace is much better." I tell her, smiling a bit, trying hard not to reveal my teeth. But somehow I think the woman in front of me knows what I am.

She puts her coffee down. Serious.

"Grace, are you injured?"

I search her eyes for any malevolence but find none. So I answer with honesty.

"Yes, ma'am. But we won't have time to fix anything right now." She reads my words with maternal worry.

"You're in danger. Ness is in danger." I nod, giving way to my own concern.

"How can I help?" She asks and I want to tell her there is nothing she can do, but think better of it.

"Do you know where she is?" She watches me tie my laces and nods.

"She went to the aquarium. I trust you know how to get there?" I nod. Why did Ness leave this house? I take my sword off the towel and sheets it to my back, fastening the worn leather buckle around my waist under the hoodie. She doesn't flinch and her eyes remain glue to my face.

Bring my girl home, please." She says and I can hear her heartbeat quicken.

"I would give my own life for hers." I tell her and mean every word. We lock eyes for another moment and then something happens I would never expect. She embraces me. Tightly. Stroking my hair as mothers do.

"Thank you." She chimes and I rush through the front door with more confusion in my head.

I hurl through the city so fast that I think my feet might give out. Fear spreads through me, bit by bit. I don't know what to do with it. What a useless feeling. A few nights ago I was ready to die, come what may. Nothing would have frightened me. I would have embraced it with open arms. Even welcomed it.

But now I have fear. Not for myself really. But for her. For this perfect being, I got to meet and know, love even? Love, another not-so-helpful feeling right now. It makes me unfocused. I met Ness' mother, who knew who, and more importantly WHAT I am. She wasn't afraid, but I've killed for less. Much less. I should have ended her. This won't end well for any of us. The deep knowledge sits in the pit of my stomach and I can't shake it.

For one I'm glad that I don't have to search the whole city for Ness. The ancient creature is far superior in strength and I don't doubt his skills exceed my own in every other area as well. I hope I am not too late. But there it is. Glowing blue against the deep grey sky of the night. It's quite pretty.

I slow my pace and examine what I see in front of me. I've learned this over the years. To watch and listen carefully when you walk into a potentially dangerous situation. Every detail matters.

189

What lays in front of me isn't even remotely subtle. The front doors are smashed through, the security system pulled straight out of the wall.

I step through fragments of glass. It crackles under my feet and I'm grateful to have my shoes back. Something must have messed with the power grid. Blue lights flash in the distance. This is backup. It's eery and quiet in the lobby. I smell it before I see it. Blood. My eyes turn silver and I spot the body behind the security desk. Hastily slain and not killed for any other reason than sport. The old security guard lies belly up on bits of broken glass that reflect the flashing blue lights. Like little stars. His chest is split, his ribcage broken and his heart ripped straight out of it. The cavernous wound stands starkly against the serenity of the blue surrounding me. His dead eyes have yet to go milky and stare at me. Blank. Another life snuffed out.

Another scent hits me and my nostrils flare. Ness. Adrenaline. I hear a yelp on my right side and have half a mind to try and bolt straight through the drywall. But I need to understand the situation first. I need to know what kind of trap I'm walking into. The short burst of pain doesn't come from Ness and the blood I smell is human, but not hers either. Regardless, I run again. Towards her. I hope I am not too late.

CHAPTER 36: DIVE - NESS

The cage is quiet. It's the name that employees and friends use for the pump room in the back of the largest tank. Thousands of water filters crowd this space with little chain-linked fenced areas separating a few of the bigger ones, hence the lovely nickname; cage. The noises are deafening. The generators are only adding to it. I wonder just how long it will take the police and the fire marshals to get here tonight. I know the moment the power grid goes off-line they're called automatically. They should be well on their way. But they might be too late for Luke and me.

We turn a corner and I halt, leaning Luke against the big step-ladder on the back of the whale shark tank. This area is off limits to the public and most employees as well. But Luke took me here when we first started dating. We made out secretly between the pumps many times. No one could hear us giggle and whisper sweet nothings into each other's ears. The thought makes me smile a bit. Luke looks exhausted and scared. He rests his injured leg against one of the big pumps and shakes his hand out. I just now get a good look at it. It's bruised from breaking the fire extinguisher free. One knuckle has a few speckles of dried blood on it. I brush over it, but he pulls away. I understand. I broke his heart just minutes ago. It seems like years have passed since.

"What is this thing?" His voice is calm but serious. His science voice, I realize. He doesn't want to talk to me, but he has to. I swallow hard and make myself look him in the eyes.

"You're not going to believe me if I tell you." My voice is equally steady as I ignore all the possible emotions bubbling up below.

A loud clink breaks my focus. It's coming from behind. We're not far ahead. We can't shake this creature. I lift Luke's arm back up without any protest and we hobble to the next pump. I can hear the water ebb and flow. The whale shark tank is the biggest in the world. Like a decent-sized lake, just glass on many sides so viewers can have a first-row seat to the secret lives of our fish friends. "This thing that's following us is something you really wished Socrates had been. Just a lot less sparkly." I tell him as I'm desperately searching for a way out for us. I feel his eyes on me but I don't dare to look. The pumps surround us, giving us decent cover, just when a hand shoots out from the darkness and clasps around his throat from behind and squeezes hard. I scream jumping to pry the long, immortal fingers off Luke's neck.

Luke chokes and wrenches desperately at the strong arm holding him.

I lock eyes with the strange, dark figure, silver eyes seemingly studying all of my human weaknesses. Luckily, I know the cage pretty well and know what happens when I press the pressure release valve to my right. It takes considerable strength and I have to take my focus off Luke for a moment, but the lever gives and moves inwards. Hot steam releases with a satisfying hiss into the dark figure's face. A SCREECH that makes my ears ring erupts from the creature but he lets go of Luke. I catch him as he staggers forward and we fumble into a sprint. We both look back and watch as the steam subsides. The immortal's face heals and turns an ashen shade of porcelain. He lowers his gaze, sniffs, and stalks after his prey; us. Luke gulps hard and looks down at me. Disbelief, wonder, I don't know for sure.

I point with my chin. Up is our only choice. The ladder is wet and slippery and Luke's leg isn't looking great, but we're out of options. If we want to get away from this monster behind us, we might have to get wet.

Luke doesn't balk at the idea and starts climbing, pulling himself up mostly with his considerable arm and upper body strength, only putting weight on his healthy leg. The high-pitched whines from the engine are the only sounds I can hear.

We reach the top and Luke grabs the big emergency harpoon, using it as a menacing walking stick. He's quite a sight as a limping, partially blood-covered, and sea-

192

water-soaked man, leaning on a harpoon for pain relief. But I don't have time to comment on it.

"Push that." He orders me and my eyes follow the direction of where he's pointing. I look behind us and without question follow his instructions and push the green button. The tank is clear and gigantic. But the moment the button's command is followed by whatever system obliges it, a cloud of fish feed is released, obstructing the view.

"If things go bad, you dive, you dive deep below the feed where it can't see you and out the other end." He tells me. Worried. I gulp. I broke his heart. This beautiful man wanted to marry me just hours ago and now, even after I've treated him so badly, he doesn't think of saving himself first but is concerned for my safety. I look across to the other end. Although his plan sounds solid, this would be an impossible task. I can't dive forty feet deep and then swim however far this might be. It's deceiving. I see myself floating, drowning in my mind, but I manage to pull myself together and follow Luke away from the ladder. We start hurrying across the narrow gangway stretching above the tank. It rattles metallic with each of our steps. Clunk.

Below us, the sea creatures awake from their slumber. Always ready for more food. Sharks of impressive size smell the blood and begin to circle. Usually looking at them from the glass tunnels is quite the calming, mesmerizing activity; up here it's vastly different.

The bridge shakes under a sudden weight. I look over my shoulder back to where we came from and lock eyes with the dark creature in pursuit. He grins, silver eyes hungry for a sadistic kill. But not at us, I realize. Past us. My eyes follow his gaze to the opposite side of the walkway.

"You're late." The monster chimes as my eyes fall on Grace. A small whimper of relief escapes me, as Luke puts a protective arm in front of me, covering me from Grace too. Instinct.

I scan her up and down and my breathing quickens. She's wearing my sweater and her pants have stains of blood on them. She's hurt. How is that possible? Her eyes shine silver and I feel Luke's fear radiating off of him. I wish I had time to explain all of this to him. Any of it.

The monster behind us scans Grace as well and chuckles in dark amusement.

"I see you've enjoyed the dinner I left behind for you. You're welcome." His voice makes the peach fuzz on my neck rise in protest. How can something sound so abhorrent?

I lock eyes with Grace who holds out a hand for us both. I try to move toward her but Luke's arm stops me in urgent worry. Of course. He doesn't know. He raises the harpoon at Grace, contemplating. She doesn't flinch.

"Stay back." He growls at her and I'm impressed. Even now, he would protect me at all costs. From anything.

"Just give me your hand." Grace pleads with him. Nothing but sincerity in her voice. She'd save him too. For me.

The monster behind us takes a leaping jump and lands much too close for my comfort, making the narrow feeding bridge sway under his immortal weight.

I cling to Luke. He holds on to me as well. Two humans stuck in a fight between two blood-thirsty creatures. Not a great place to be.

"Now!"

Grace implores Luke with her eyes. Blue and silver pulsing through them. Switching. What happened to her? She seems not entirely in control of herself.

Luke sighs, conflicted. He glances behind us where the monster is inching closer as though he had all the time in the world. I suppose he does. It's us who struggle much more with the concept of time.

Luke reluctantly reaches out a hand and Grace pulls him behind her in one swift motion. She yelps at the tug in her shoulder. Pain, I realize and she avoids my gaze. Pain? How can that be? I take a step forward, reaching my hand out to both of them when the monster behind me pounces. One agile jump is all it takes and he lands right behind me. Both of us mere feet from Grace and Luke.

194

I stiffen with cold dread. The dark figure slides a hand across my waist. Disgust shoots through me. He smells foul. Like decay and cruelty. The other hand freely explores the locks of my hair. Playing with them. Scratching my scalp. I shiver and close my eyes, freezing into stillness.

Luke angles the harpoon at the monster, determination distorting his normally perfect features.

"Stake through the heart? Poetic but a little cliché." The monster says with a mocking tone. He's so very close to me. His body presses against my mine. I can feel his thighs. Solid and unyielding. Honed from stone, not flesh.

The dark figure smells my neck, running his nose and lips across my skin. It feels like sandpaper. He hums in sensual approval and I shudder. This is it. I will die today. With a lover's purr, he whispers into my ear.

"Do you think his aim is good enough? Because mine certainly is." He croons and plunges his fangs into the soft skin of my neck.

I scream and shake, looking at both Luke and Grace, who can only watch in sheer horror as the monster gorges himself on my flowing blood. I feel it drain out of me in small bursts, bolstered by the immortal's strength. I hear him laugh out loud as he tightens his grip on my waist and lets us fall into the water.

The image of Luke's harpoon flashes by me in a split second. Did he hit the creature? Did he hit me? I don't feel much but the cold embrace of the deep. I'm going to die today.

CHAPTER 37: UNDERWATER - GRACE

I tear the sweater off me and hand it to the perplexed human man I'm standing next to. I jump into the tank without a second thought. What have I done? My search for answers has likely killed the person I love. The cold water hits me and enters the wound on my shoulder with merciless cruelty. It stings like a million little shards of glass but I ignore it.

I have to dive past the cloud of fish feed, pulling myself through with only one arm. Schools of shiny little creatures float past me as if in greeting. My gaze follows them in hopes of spotting Ness. But I don't see her anywhere. A current nuzzles me from behind and almost bumps into my injured shoulder as a large shark pays me no regard, in search of tastier endeavors. It startles me regardless.

I swim, scanning the depths for any sign of Ness or the monster I've come to hate. Nothing.

I continue down, feeling the water pressure increase with every stroke. The rock formation in front of me obstructs my view so I pull myself closer to peak around it. There. The monster is already smiling at me. Sneering hideously from ear to ear, as if he'd been waiting long and I was late for proper tea.

Rage courses through my veins and I push faster. Through the murky, blood-clouded water towards that thing, I have to kill. I thought I was the worst this world had to offer, a creature whose only existence was to murder and feed, with no way out, but this is one beast that outshines any of my darkest hours. He hurts, maims, and kills for sport whenever he pleases. I think he might even enjoy every second of it, never having had a conscious. I can't allow it to continue on. I shudder at the thought of the family ties. My uncle. I'm related to it. Even worse, my father was a killer too. For all his knowledge of medicine and healing, how many innocent people died because of him? Was he like this monster?

Did he end humans cruelly? Or did he try his best to put a kind end to only what he needed?

I have so many questions. The villagers burning our house down, calling us the devil and devil's spawn had been right. We were the monsters. I don't like the spiral of revelations I'm going down one bit and I push through the pain back into reality, closer to the dark figure floating ahead, when suddenly-

A large, dark shadow cuts off my path. Consuming my entire line of sight, the whale shark passes unhurriedly with slow grace like a dancer leaping in outer space. I marvel at it and all of its small, white dots.

As it clears my view, all I can see is a small school of colorful fish darting back and forth, no looming creature of death, no Ness.

Somehow I've reached the bottom of the tank and it truly feels like the ocean floor. Small clouds of sand billow up where my feet land. Schools of fish dance through the currents. But I don't see the monster. I look up. A figure is silhouetted against the blue lights illuminating the tank from above. Face down. Ness. I push off the ground as hard as my feet allow and shoot through the depths. My one good arm makes it an arduous endeavor of willpower. But there she is. I see her fingers twitch. Still alive. But she's slumped forward, face down in the water with large predators and a few sharks to boot. A few more feet and I'll reach the surface. The light shines brighter up here. It's much easier to see. I can make out Ness' facial features. Too relaxed for my liking. I focus on my senses, eyes turning silver, and hear a slow heartbeat. Still alive.

My hand breaks the surface just as a sharp pain shoots through me with cruel precision. Cold steel with a barbed arrow point burrows through my side and rears its ugly head out of my lower back. I instinctively try to suck in air, but only get a lung full of saltwater. I choke on it and my throat burns. My silver eyes sputter and I manage to turn to see the dark figure near a familiar rock formation.

He impaled me with the large harpoon and he still holds the rope it's tied to. My blood bubbles through the water. This is it. I won't reach Ness. I feel myself weakening. Immortality waning with every passing second. I come to realize that there is indeed no such thing as true eternal life.

The monster yanks the rope and like a dog on a leash, my body obliges his command. His preternatural strength pulls me back down and fast. I steal one last glance at Ness. One last glimpse at the idea of what could have been.

CHAPTER 38: TOGETHER - LUKE

I still can't quite believe it. I've dedicated my entire career to finding and studying a way to beat death as a disease. I always thought that we, as a species, could master it and create a peaceful society in which everyone has a chance to live out all of their dreams with all the time in the world.

Now I'm being hunted by one immortal creature while watching another bleed in the deep blue of the aquarium and it makes me think I got it all wrong. Their intrinsic state seems to be like that of a true sickness, an ailment which nothing can cure. I shuffle, trying to spot Ness but my injured leg doesn't make it easy. I ignore the pain with mediocre success and continue scanning the choppy surface of the water. We have a wonderful, modern machine imitating actual waves and I curse it under my breath. I can't see her anywhere.

Below I spot movement. The feeding frenzy is driving the creatures wild a second time in one day. Sharks circle and little schools of fish scatter apart to not be in the way of giant, teeth-filed maws. I can't see the two humanoid monsters and I don't much care to.

There, on the far side of the tank, I spot something floating. Ness. Her wet hair is tangled around her head and she's face down. My heart drops.

Without a second thought, I dive head first and let the coolness pool around me as I let my dread propel me toward her. I'm not an athlete, but I will drive myself forward when it counts. No matter what happened between us, I love her and will always love Ness. Whatever creatures below me loom to take us both, I would give my life for her. So I swim as fast as I can, pushing my body to the brink. I can feel it protesting. The salt sneaks its biting way into my wound and stings with unrelenting fervor.

Shadows of beasts outmatching both my skill and hunger close in from all sides. I've never had a fear of sharks, but seeing a dorsal fin breach and accompany me in perfect unison isn't exactly a sign of camaraderie. I am prey. My primary skillset of logic and determined studying doesn't exactly come in handy in this element. I am food and nothing more. The largest of the looming shadows bows below again and bends, most certainly to circle in for an attack. But I will ignore that entirely. I reach Ness and turn her limp body over. Her jaw hangs slack and her eyes are closed. Her skin has fallen ashen and is almost grey around the two puncture wounds on her neck. But she is still warm. I don't have time to examine her properly. We need to get out of the water. Out of our beloved, usually relaxing aquarium.

Luckily, the feeding bridge stretches across the entirety of the tank and isn't too far away. I scoop Ness under one arm and push through the artificial waves with all of my remaining strength. I ignore any and all monsters beneath us and breathlessly manage to hoist Ness' lifeless body onto the scaffolding with the last ounce of strength in my body. I struggle to sit myself up on the gangway and drag her upper body out of the water, then I lift her legs out. We've made it. Without hesitation, I check to see if she's breathing. I lower my ear to her mouth. I can't tell. The sloshing water and my own exhaustion have dulled my senses. I softly pat Ness' cheek but now is not the time to be gentle, I realize, and start pumping her chest with well-practiced CPR movements. Fingers interlaced and shoulders squared, I push what feels like too hard, down on her sternum. Steady and not letting up. I count out loud to set a rhythm. Then I open her mouth, head tilted back, and breathe air into her lungs. I repeat the process with sheer determination. Fear spreads through me but I don't let up. No. She can't be gone. I push again, harder. I've heard about people breaking ribs during this process, but actually doing it feels so dehumanizing. I shudder.

I breathe into her mouth again, the act is intimate and very foreign all at the same time.

"C'mon. We have a fight to finish." I order her and she must agree because her eyes fly open, she twists to the side and coughs out an impressive amount of saltwater.

The utter relief floors me and I slump down on my ass, taking in a few deep breaths.

After what seems like hours, limping through the tunnels away from the tank and its looming danger, Ness and I finally make it to my car. She must have hyperthermia. She's so still and drained. She can barely speak and her fingers have not yet uncurled. My worry makes me race through the Atlanta traffic with the urgency of a first-time bank robber. The lights blur by. Cars and buildings alike but I pay them no mind. My entire focus is on Ness.
Both of our phones are rendered useless. Ness' is likely on the bottom of the tank or in some whale shark's belly, mine has given up due to death by water exposure. I don't blame it.
"Get me to...Mom." She gets out weakly and my concern grows as I fiddle with the seat-heating button. It's not enough.
"I'm driving you to the hospital." I tell her, watching her eyes flare up in what I can only assume is fear. She seems to be very out of it, phasing in and out of reality. I'm not sure what she's going through.
"No. Please...Mom." She begs me and I half-heartedly agree. She doesn't have the words to explain it, but it's not just the almost drowning that would come to light. She literally drank my research and was bitten in the neck by that...THING. If I say it out loud it makes it real, I think to myself. It can't be. Right? It cannot possibly be real. I'm a scientist. There has to be a logical, straightforward, and simple explanation for this.

It's almost morning when I half carry Ness up the steps to her mother's house on my injured leg. I have become very good at ignoring my own pain. Beth opens the door before I can even knock, seemingly prepared for this strange eventuality. She ushers us inside the kitchen and I follow through.
I prop Ness onto a chair and Beth starts shining a flashlight into each pupil checking her daughter's vitals.

Ness shies away from the lights as if they were a bee sting. The tea kettle is already whining, ready with warmth.

"You said she almost drowned?" Beth asks her professional medical tone a tool I've never seen her use.

I nod and also pull Ness' hair back to show the wound on her neck.

"Yes, but there should be a decent amount of blood loss as well. Something...bit her." I stammer, but Beth doesn't lose a beat. She examines the neck, which is somehow perfectly pristine and without any bite marks to be found. Her skin is greying but intact.

I blink and wonder whether or not I imagined it. Any of it. Maybe we just fought and she fell into the tank? I have heard that drowning can give you hallucinations. Maybe that happened to me? But I shift my stance and can feel my injured leg, throbbing pain still very much present and sobering. No. This was indeed real. All of it.

Ness groans as Beth checks her blood pressure. She frowns at the results.

"It's a bit low, but she'll be ok. Let's warm her up. Keep rubbing her arms with the towel." Doctors always sound calm, even in the face of true adversity. So I'm not a hundred percent certain that Ness will be ok. But I follow the instructions and rub her arms inch by inch with a soft, fluffy towel as Beth feeds her spoons full of hot tea.

"What happened to her?" She asks very carefully, avoiding my eyes. She knows something.

"I don't even know whether I want to say it out loud. That would make it real." I tell her and her eyes find mine. Maternal concern and pity in them.

Tasting the tea, Ness gags, and bunches over. Beth checks to see if it's the temperature, but she has no problem with it. Now I'm even more worried. She was bitten. By that...THING. But before I can complete any thoughts I hear a loud THUD on the roof. Like something heavy having landed. All three pairs of eyes jump up as if we could look through the three floors between the kitchen and the sky. STEPS. Clear as day.

Beth pins me down with a stern look.

"Stay here." She orders me. She walks to the cabinet near the fridge and pulls her gun out. I blink in surprise and in awe. I've never seen this side of her.

"There is a second one in my nightstand, go grab it." She continues and I nod. I love her even more. What a badass.

"No." Ness pipes weakly and my arm instinctively holds her tightly around her shoulders.

"It's all right. We're here." I tell her, hoping it'll comfort her.

"Don't let her go." She rasps and I see the worry in her eyes. Color returns to Ness' cheeks as she lifts herself from the chair. She's shaky and resembles a newborn deer.

"Take it easy, Babe." I tell her, realizing the use of the pet name too late. Habit. Our eyes meet briefly and without words, we agree that this is a topic for a later conversation.

"Can you please check on my mom? What if it followed..." She doesn't have to finish the sentence for my face to fall. I know what she means by IT. I nod at her. As much as I hate leaving her alone in the kitchen, it'll only be a moment. She's survived worse tonight.

I lean heavily on the banister. For a few moments, I forgot about my own pain. Well, three flights of stairs are more than happy to remind me of its full glory. It shoots all the way up my spine into my head. I should probably check on that. Later.

I step into Ness' small attic room. The window is open and the curtains are blowing in the wind. I came just in time to watch Beth close them tightly.

"Nothing?" I ask her as I scan the room myself, even bending to check under the bed. It makes me wince in pain.

"Only the window. Must have burst open with the wind." She says resolutely. It sounds confident but I give the room another once over. After this night, nothing would entirely surprise me.

"Let's check your leg, shall we?" She ushers me out of the room but I can't shake the feeling that we are not alone in this house. The door shuts behind us and I think I hear another step inside. I'm about to ask her for the gun when the doorbell rings brightly in stark contrast to the events of the night.

CHAPTER 39: DUST AND DAYLIGHT - GRACE

I'm pinned. Saying it's between a rock and a hard place would be putting it lightly. The monster had pulled me all the way back down to the little, artificial coral reef and then hooked the bulky harpoon into the rocks. I watched his wretched face go blurry as he floated away in utter amusement. His form got distorted by the waves that also carried my small trail of blood to our fellow predators who call these waters home.

I'm a hunter, an alpha in my own right. I never thought I had to compete with or fear a shark. This was so far off my radar of possible outcomes for my intended ending, I want to laugh at myself. I wriggle against the steel of the weapon but it doesn't budge. In the distance I watch a large shadow pick up my scent and slowly change direction. I do not want to be its dinner. I wrench more, chafing the skin on my back against the sharp corals. I scream in the deep but my desperation is heard by no one. Ness' form isn't floating on the surface anymore. I can only hope that the human man I feel considerable jealousy about managed to pick her up and get her to safety. Otherwise, I might kill him just for stupidity and uselessness.

I squeeze down and feel my back grating against the stone but I have to get out of this predicament. Fast. Whatever decided to want to come pay me a visit is coming closer with elegant speed and a mouth full of very large teeth. Bigger than mine. I twist against the sharp metal and break the harpoon in two. Finally, I twist my neck and manage to free myself. Without much reprieve, I start swimming up. I do my best with considerable injuries that refuse to knit back together and heal as they usually do. I glance behind me and the shark is still in pursuit, albeit not at full speed. A smaller fish did me a solid favor and got in his way, as an appetizer or a distraction, depending on how fast I manage to leave this hellish water.

I've decided I don't care much for aquariums anymore as I manage to pull myself out slowly onto the ladder. I lie there and stare at the ceiling for just a beat, drenched in gore and fish guts. At least the blood has been washed off decently. It's the small things in life we should be grateful for. I sit up and scan around me. The monster is gone and so are Ness and her human...friend. I have to pull myself together quickly and track their scent. I have to be quicker than my fellow immortal beast.

I stagger to my feet, every injury making me acutely aware of what I am not anymore; invincible.

I limp through the broken front door, leaving behind complete chaos. The fresh morning air hits me with a new threat; quickly approaching daylight. I hurry through the parking lot, just when the sirens finally make an appearance. I don't know what kind of security system this place has, but it needs a dramatic overhaul. It took the police and the fire trucks way too long to get here and be of use.

I manage to slip through the shadow and stumble forward into a run. I press my injured hand to the wound in my side, trying to stop the blood from flowing. It's quite an odd sensation. Leaking life. I half-smile at the realization, aware of every fleeting moment.

There is it, Ness' familiar, unmistakable scent. She's not doing well either. My eyes change to silver and I pick up some speed. Not enough I realize. A few bends and turns and I know. Another scent is near. My uncle. He found them before I did. He followed them, likely to deliver their bodies to me. The thought makes me feel sick to my stomach.

Behind me, I spot a first, annoyingly inconvenient ray of sunshine. Two more blocks and I will be there. Two more blocks and I can walk up the steps of Ness' house and hold her.

The pagan statue of the buck-man gleams in front of the old library. It's still wet from last night's rain and steadily becoming shinier with daylight. I can make it. I ignore the pain and will my body to run faster.

But I struggle. Almost there. The light comes up quickly. I can feel it on my heels.

No, no, no. My skin shines and prickles with the sensation. Not now, I think as dust evaporates from me. Pain ripples through me and then I burn into millions of little particles being carried away by the wind.

CHAPTER 40: WALLS CLOSING IN - NESS

I feel a little more steady on my legs as the warmth finally returns to my body. A sliver of daylight creeps through the kitchen window from behind me and I think that renders us fairly safe from any nighttime beasts and monsters. The doorbell chimes a second time and I hear a muffled, low voice out front. I sway forward with slow determination. The wall is my friend.

Both my mother and Luke rush down the stairs and hover behind me.

"Don't open it." Luke huffs with no small amount of panic in his voice. But it's too late. I've already pushed down the handle and the hinges swing inwards, revealing my boss, Matt with a face I cannot read. Shame maybe? I angle my head to make him look at me, but his eyes avoid mine. He's accompanied by two police officers and now I'm officially freaked out. All three are somber. One of the officers even takes off his hat and wipes his shoes. My eyes dart from one to the next as my heart quickens with concern. What is this?

"You look like you still haven't slept." Matt notes and I blink back a retort. Sorry, I'm currently not my cheery, fresh-faced self, but I suppose he's right. I've kinda been busy the past two nights and pretty much ignored the need to sleep almost entirely. Somehow I don't feel the fatigue.

"I haven't." I say simply and let him say whatever he needs to. Matt looks to Luke and Beth, both on edge as well. Then back to me. This waiting for the other shoe-to-drop-thing is making me very anxious and I'm about to burst.

"What is this?" I ask not directed at any of them in particular. Are they here to collect me? Place me on a temporary 5150 mental hold and evaluate me? I wouldn't entirely blame any of them. Maybe it's an intervention? But I'm not a drug user. I'm just very confused. One of the officers hands me a neatly folded, velvet letter envelope. The paper is soft and beautiful. Delicate even.

211

On the outside, written in beautiful script is 'Ness, Lifeline'.

"It's just protocol, ma'am." Did he just call me Ma'am? Oh boy, I must look absolutely ghastly. I pin my attention on Matt, asking with every inch of my being.

"Matt? Tell me." I order him. I'm tired of this soft waiting period. He nods and a heavy sigh escapes him. This is hard for him, and I realize that whatever is about to come out of his mouth, I won't like it. I'm right.

"There is no good way to say this." He begins and he tries to take my hand. I let him. He's always been there for me. His kindness and guidance; a shining light in our strange profession.

"Yesterday, Emma, your recurring caller, finally reported her father to the police for battery. They answered the call promptly and were on their way to her house immediately. Did everything by the book." He pauses and I already know how this story ends. I retract my hand, starting to shake my head, willing the final words to be different, but he continues on.

"When they got to the house, Emma had taken her own life." The words hang in the air, heavy and deafening. No, no, no, no. I gulp in air, almost hyperventilating. My mom steps closer to me and places a comforting hand on my shoulder that I can barely feel. No, not Emma. Not that beautiful, innocent, vibrant soul. She was supposed to get through this. I was supposed to pull her up. I was her light at the end of the tunnel. But I wasn't there, I realize in horror and thick tears build up so quickly that I don't even have a chance to cover them up. I don't care to.

"Did she call in yesterday?" I ask, unsure if I really want to know. Matt hesitates, also uncertain if he should tell me, whether it would even help. He wipes his eyes as well. This is hitting him just as hard.

"She just left you this letter." I look at the soft paper in my shaking hand. It's yellow. A pretty, light shade that reminds me of Easter. It suits her. Suited her.

"I apologize, we have to open and copy them for evidence." One of the officers says and I can tell he feels terrible for having to be part of this mess. I swallow down whatever sobs I can, but my tears plop freely to the floor. "Did she call?" I ask one more time, pinning Matt down with my gaze.

He clamps his jaw shut tightly, trying his best to think through the small trails of tears on his own face.

"Did she?" My voice breaks and I see his shallow nod.

"Yes." He says with shattering finality.

Emma is gone and I wasn't there to help her. I lift the envelope and try to will my hands to calm as I take out a single sheet of silky paper. I can't look at any of them and step away a bit, to the stairs.

I scoff at the words, so familiar, so silly, and now so very stupid. Then I toss the letter into the trash bin and rush upstairs. Away from the pitiful faces, reading every emotion and trying to console me, make me feel better about a death I could have helped to avoid.

Behind me, I hear my mother rummage through the bin and fish out the paper.

"What does it say?" Luke asks, his voice kind and collected.

My eyes squeeze shut. I am holding on to the door to my room, still listening.

"It's a poem." My mother tells them with a level of confusion.

"Last night upon the stair,
I saw a girl who wasn't there.
She wasn't there again today.
Oh how I wish, she'd go away."

Silence. In the hallway and down below, but not in my head. I enter my room and start pacing back and forth in the cramped quarters as if that would change anything. I had shared that poem with Emma once and we had discussed the deep meaning behind each word before coming to the conclusion that sometimes, just sometimes, we don't have to overthink everything. She did it. She ended her life and broke another piece off of my already shattered heart. I didn't think it could break any more. Within two nights, it's lost so many pieces. I try to feel it pump blood through my veins, try to center myself around its simple function, but my head pounds with a much-deserved headache.

All my emotions come up at once. Anger seems to be next. How could she? If I was able, I'd bring her back to life, slap her across her pretty face and tell her to just live through a few more hard years before getting to claim and own a gorgeous, free life for herself. I was trained for this, for dealing with suicide and loss. But this one hits so hard that I don't know what to do with myself. As a counselor, I'd tell myself that all of those thoughts are very normal and that I should acknowledge and feel them. There is no wrong emotion. Somehow those sentences make me angrier and I want to break something. I see my cup of tea on my nightstand, I pick it up and hurl it against the wall. It doesn't even have the courtesy to shatter. It just clinks and falls to the ground untouched, spilling the tea bag. That is incredibly dissatisfying.

A knock takes me out of my emotional misery and before I have time to answer, Luke comes in and sweeps me into a tight hug. I don't fight it. I don't want to. He guides us to my bed and I curl into him, spilling my tears against his strong chest.

For minutes we don't speak. He just holds me gently, pats my hair, and then kisses the top of my head like he used to do. The first touch of his lips feels nice. Like a comfort. He knows me so well, has seen me at my worst, and yet, he chooses to be here and love me in this way. Then he tilts my head back to look at me and wipes my tears away with the stroke of his thumbs. He kisses my cheeks. Each one and I realize I'm entering a prison of a different kind. I try to take his hands, not ready for this, not ready to have this conversation NOW. But he tries to kiss my lips and claim me. I turn away and stop him cold, but that doesn't seem to be enough.

"We can fix this." He says and I know he doesn't mean Emma. He means us. Our relationship. This beautiful, kind-hearted man has no sensibility for timing. He continues.

"Us. We can fix us. I understand. It wasn't your fault. That thing...it just overcame you." His words are full of understanding I neither deserve nor want. It feels like he's pressing me against the walls of a cage. I stare at him blankly and for a moment, my tears for Emma subside.

"We can work on us and fight for it. Our love." His eyes search mine for the smallest glimmer of hope and I know what I have to do. Kindness isn't actually kind. It prolongs and tortures and twists a dull knife into a gaping wound. So I decide to forgo that entirely and break one more heart tonight beyond repair.

"You should go." I tell him with finality. I know it needs to be this way. But he looks at me with a sense of shock.

"There's no fixing anything. One of my callers just died and I feel responsible. You can't fix that." I tell him. My words don't sound cruel. They are direct and straightforward, but I watch them land like a direct missile. I continue.

"You can't bring her back. You can't bring back my father either. People leave. They die. They always die. You're so obsessed with fixing everything that you don't understand that some things are just meant to be broken." The air feels cold now. I hear myself. I sound different. I wouldn't blame him if he never speaks to me again. That doesn't mean I won't always love him in some way. I will. But this isn't right. I rise to my feet.

"This thing with Grace was my decision. She didn't make me do anything. I love her." I tell him and I watch the final crack crawl all the way down the surface of his pure heart and tear it asunder. It's a terrible thing to watch. But I'm numb. It's been too much. Too many things have built onto one another for me to feel this moment. I am empty.

215

He gets up, his face flat and drained of any visible emotion.

"You're pushing away the best thing in your life to be with that...thing?" I look at him one more time. He's the person I grew up into an adult with. He's my closest friend. He's part of my soul. But in this moment, the love has forever changed.

"She's going to kill you." He states with concern but no ire.

I smile sadly. Another tear down my face as I nod. He might not be wrong. He leaves me to my own devices and I hear the lock shut forever as he exits and takes that beautiful idea of a perfect life with him.

I need to center myself. So I grab my comically large, noise-canceling headphones and put on some music as I lay down. Whether it will lull me to sleep, or just distract me, I will take both or either without any specific preference. I am empty.

CHAPTER 41: STILL HERE

Luke rushes down the stairs, his steps heavy with the loss. Without looking anywhere but his feet, he bursts through the front door and lets it fall into the heavy lock.
BAM.

From the kitchen, Beth turns for a moment, a heavy sigh escaping her as she cleans a coffee cup over the sink.
Another few steps click behind her into the kitchen.
"Didn't I just hear you leaving?" She says without turning around.
A voice old and unfamiliar answers her, freezing her thoughts in their tracks.
"That wasn't me." The ancient monster croons and approaches a bit closer, invading her space with a threatening sense of curiosity.
"I've actually been here for quite a while now. Watching and listening." Beth turns to look at the owner of this unpleasant accent and stares into a pair of strange, silver eyes.

"You were on the roof." She says matter-of-factly and he smiles at her, letting his long nails scratch slowly across the kitchen table, leaving an easy indentation. Pure strength in small movements.
"Beautiful home. Very inviting indeed." He continues on and Beth can't stand the sound and presence of him.
She scans the kitchen as subtly as she can. Her gun is on the other side, behind the dark creature. He leans against the fridge and sniffs the air.
"So many different scents in here." He hums in pleasure, enjoying every 's' with all the sensual sweetness of brackish swamp water.
Beth's heart races. She's trying not to glimpse at the gun, for fear of giving away her plan.
"What do you want?" Her voice holds steady.
The monster smiles. Easy and a little too casual.
"I want to mark my territory."

He pounces. Wicked and quick. One jump and Beth hits the ground hard. Her head slams against the table leg and she flails her arms in an attempt to cover herself. She yelps as a sharp knife slices her arm, shooting searing pain through her body. She dares a look and blood sprouts from the bend of her elbow all the way to the wrist. As a doctor, she knows what this means and how much time she has left before bleeding out.

Beth spits in the creature's face and punches him in the jaw with the other hand as hard as she can.

The dark figure rises, inhaling sharply. Enjoying this. Beth scoots backward, cradling her arm, looking for anything to help defend herself.

The dark figure smirks. He steps back a few feet and her eyes follow him as he picks up the pistol, her way out, and hands it butt-first to her. She blinks in disbelief.

"Would this make you feel safer?" He croons and his eyes glow in their unnatural silver might. Beth understands. She levels the gun at him anyway. The bastard even has the arrogance to spread his arms wide, giving her perfect aim. She pulls the trigger down, but the weapon only clicks. Empty magazine.

The monster chuckles.

"Well, if it makes you feel any better, it wouldn't have done the trick anyway." He educates her like a child, watching every move, playing with her like a cat would with a mouse.

Beth tosses the gun at him and gets to her feet. Blood dripping heavily from her arm, but she continues staring the creature down in an act of final defiance.

"No screams? No begging?" He asks, cocking his head with interest that could almost resemble respect.

"Is that what gets you off?" She shoots back, trying to rattle his cage.

Beth twists sideways, jumps toward the window, and rips the curtains open. Rain and gloomy daylight greet her. But it affects the monster nonetheless.

A HISS erupts from him as he steps back. Eyes shining.

A barrier of light between them. The understanding of just what he is fully settles within Beth as her mind works through possible solutions. She can kill it, or at least slow it down with sunlight. If she can get the monster to the door, then she just might have a chance.

The dark figure smirks at her as if reading her mind. Then he slowly takes a step. Steam and pain ripple off of him but he clenches his jaw, working his way through the detrimental daylight. Another step. Parts of him ripple. Beth can only watch as he passes through to the other side and heals immediately.
"You're clever, but a little ray of light won't kill someone of my strength either."
Beth retreats another step. Blood covers the floor. She scrambles behind her, throwing anything she can at the dark figure. The hot tea kettle, plates, cutlery, the phone, and an unfortunate basil plant. But the few hits she manages to get in don't affect the ancient creature. He lets her attack subside and then pounces, inflicting another vicious slice, this time to Beth's neck.
He jumps to the other corner of the kitchen to watch her struggle and fight off her impending doom.
Beth gulps. A large, vertical wound on her neck, neatly bisecting her carotid artery, causes blood to stream freely and rapidly. Her eyes widen as if she'd like to say something, but her injury prevents her from doing so.
She tries to staunch the blood from flowing, but now both arms are sliced. He's bleeding her out bit by bit. She takes a step towards the figure and slips in her own blood. She falls and crashes, trying desperately to breathe before her injuries drown her in her own blood. Her hands fruitlessly search for something, anything, to hold onto, but all she can feel is her warm, wet blood smeared all across the kitchen floor. She stares up at the dark figure who bends down to caress her hair with a strange tenderness.
"Would you like me to end it for you?" He asks, sounding almost empathetic.

She chokes on her own blood again. Another jolt rattles through her broken body and her eyes glaze over. Her body stills into the all-encompassing oblivion of death. The monster continues to stroke Beth's hair and even wipes a few strands off of her cheek.

"I guess I won't have to." He says to the corpse and rises in one fluid motion, ready to continue his hunt. His nostrils flare just slightly and his eyes dart to the staircase leading to Ness' room. He hums to himself, savoring each second in sweet anticipation.

He saunters upwards, taking in every family picture on the wall, smiling at the happy humans. He daintily avoids the small rays of light through the curtains with loathsome distaste. He halts in front of Ness' door, letting every detail to become a part of his Michelin Star dining experience. His fingertips delicately glide along the outside, tracing the adornments in the wood.

Then the monster kicks the door in without any trouble. One smooth movement. But instead of a playful, cruel hunt, an open window greets him and daylight floods the room. A loud shriek escapes the creature and he jumps to cower into the nearest, darkest corner to hide in the shadows. The dust settles. No Ness anywhere. Only the abominable, open window with flowing curtains letting in gloomy daylight.

Another scream erupts from the monster. Pain and hatred combined in one wretched sound of frustration.

CHAPTER 42: EARLY GOODBYE - NESS

I couldn't sleep. Even after days of complete deprivation, hardly any food, and intense emotional upheaval, I was unable to drift off. Maybe I don't deserve it anymore. The sweet feeling of dulling comfort. Listening to music also didn't relax me. My mind continued to bounce off of one thought straight to the next and I simply didn't want to just lay there any longer torturing myself. But I also couldn't face my mother. The idea of going down to the kitchen and having her look at me, comfort me after breaking Luke's heart and after receiving Emma's letter didn't sit right. I am not ready to talk about anything. Not yet. So I did the only sensible thing and went out the window.

Turns out that route is a lot more difficult than I had imagined. The slanted roof was fairly easy to scoot down on, but then I was a bit stuck. It's still a three-story building and I'd never done anything like this before. So, I inched myself over until the gutters connected with the downspout on the side of the house, right alongside the kitchen window. I turned over and lowered myself, legs first. Finding hold on a normal day would have likely been quite difficult. Between the rain, my state of mind, and lack of sleep, I've truly managed to pick a challenge. Thankfully, the bolts holding the pipe to the bricks give me enough grip to start moving down bit by bit. My arms burned with the strain, but it worked.
I neared the kitchen and saw light emanating from it. I paused for a moment and heard my mother speaking with someone. It was muffled but sounded intense. She was using her professional tone and I didn't want to give her any reason to direct it at me. I clung on even tighter to the pipe and inched a bit lower. Just in time, it turns out, because Mom suddenly yanked open the curtains at the kitchen window. Did she hear me? Impossible. Before I could give her another chance to discover her adult daughter sneaking out of the house to avoid a comforting

conversation, I took a leap of faith and let myself fall the remainder of the way down. I landed on my ass but miraculously didn't hurt myself in any way. Good.

With a pounding heart that usually accompanies a prison break of this magnitude, I rushed around the corner. I knew exactly where I wanted to go today, even though it wouldn't make my sorrow disappear. In fact, just the opposite.
Emma had told me so many abhorrent stories about her dad. I don't even fully blame her for wanting to end her life. I understand. But I know that those moments in life pass with the right support. I halt at that thought and suck in a cold breath of winter air. I should have been her support. I know it was still her decision. All my training tells me this isn't my fault and I can't take it on. And yet, I wasn't there for her when it really mattered. I had my head stuck up my own ass, breaking Luke's heart and chasing monsters. The person she relied on in her darkest hour wasn't there. I continue on, into her neighborhood. I know where Emma lives. She shared every detail of her life with me for the past eighteen months or so. I also remember her telling me that her father would want to erase her, as she put it, as quickly as possible. The stain she brought on her family. He called her that as a nickname; Stain. I remember hearing that the first time we spoke and it rendering me utterly speechless. The lack of empathy and compassion. I really wanted to slap her father into reality even back then. Regardless of whether or not he agreed with his child's transition into a woman, love should have won out. But we're in the South after all. We're surrounded by so much fear and traditional pressure that love and fear are mixed up on a daily basis. Emma told me once, that if she ever died, her father would want her funeral to be that day. She was certain. Just to be done with it and give the neighbors zero chance to mourn the real her. He wouldn't want any of her freak friends to come, dressed up as women, and embarrass him. I see the little New Hope Baptist Church stick out

222

like a sore thumb and have to raise my brows at the name and the immediate reference jumping to mind. I wonder how many nerds drive by this place and quietly hum the Imperial March, imitating Darth Vader. I hope it's a great number.

In sad discomfort, I realize I was right to hurry.

The service must have just finished. Pictures of Emma as a boy are propped up on large stands. Flowers. White and clean. It's like her family knew she would die soon and had a plan in place. I remember her telling me her father didn't discourage the suicide, rather than having her become an embarrassment for him during Thanksgiving. The thought freezes any sympathy for her closest relatives within my heart. I didn't think I could ever truly hate someone, well, I might just learn a new skill today.

Only the funeral director, a plump man in his forties with professional comfort eyes, is still near the casket. He eyes me with curiosity. I don't quite fit in, I suppose. I fold my hands and try to ignore him, but he addresses me directly.

"The service just ended. The family will join the lowering of the casket in half an hour if you would like to give your condolences." He is kind. It seems genuine.

I step up still not answering the man. The coffin is clunky. A dark brown monstrosity with deep blue velvet sprouting from it. Nothing feminine about it.

Emma looks like a stranger. Made up in a suit and tie. Her hair is cut short. Coiffed into prep-school proper. This isn't her. This wax figure-looking thing has her face and delicate hands, but it doesn't come close to who she was in life. They took her life from her long before she died, I realize and tears fall from my eyes. I sob, not being able to control myself. I don't care. I don't know the man beside me. But my tears fall into Emma's casket onto her made-up, painted hands. They wash away a little bit of the absurdly beige paint on her skin, a bit of ashen truth left behind.

"Oh, Emma." I hear myself saying, sounding like a proper widow. The funeral director blinks in confusion. "Ma'am, are you here for Michael Payton?"

I sigh heavily. I had forgotten Emma's legal name a while ago. It feels so strange to hear it. Michael Payton was supposed to grow up and play football in school. He was supposed to go All-American and at least get himself a nice little Division 1 scholarship to a decent out-of-state college. He was meant to come home for Christmas and tell his father about his latest conquests over a beer or two, all the while excelling at business or law or anything else that's decently useful. Micheal Payton was supposed to marry after school and cover up an affair or two in his life, get a good job, a solid car and pat his father on the back when they went tubing every summer. That was the life laid out for the name that couldn't possibly fit Emma any less.

Emma was artistic and brilliant. She could see things others couldn't and felt more intensely than most people I've met. She listened well and truthfully and had a strong sense of integrity. Emma was beautiful and would have made an amazing artist, wife, and mother.

Without hesitation, I reach down into her casket and ruffle her perfectly coiffed hair. A little rebellion is most certainly necessary. Better.

"Her name was Emma. She would have hated this." I tell the man next to me and I see his face change in true understanding.

"You're gonna close the casket, right? Her family won't see her again?" I ask, not entirely sure what I'm getting ready to do here. But he only nods, letting me decide whatever comes next. I bend down and take the tie off Emma's neck and pocket it. She hated ties unless she wore them as a belt.

"Don't tell on me." I request. But he does me one better than just to promise. The funeral director takes a turquoise hair tie from his wrist and puts it on Emma's hand. My broken heart aches from tenderness.

"I have a three-year-old daughter." He tells me and my sobs come out even harder, twisting my face into true sorrow.

224

"She'll be at plot 47." He tells me and I try to nod. His comforting hand on my shoulder is a steady weight. This man doesn't just fulfill his duty with his job, he's meant to help people grieve.

I am very confused as to what time of day it is. The sun is hiding behind a thick cover of clouds. If I squint, I can make out its outline already hanging very low to the horizon. The cemetery is small and old. Like out of a book on Southern history. My steps crunch through the grass. It's gotten so cold outside that the grass is covered in frost. I can see my breath cloud before me as I exhale. The small group is far off and I find myself a seat on an icy bench. I don't care much for comfort today. I watch them fidget as Emma's coffin is lowered into the earth. They're all uncomfortable. Somehow that doesn't feel like it's nearly enough. A middle-aged woman, likely Emma's mother, throws a white rose atop. I huff a bit. The sight just makes me even angrier.

Emma's father, the man from all of her awful stories is a middle-aged mustache lover with cruel eyes. I spot him from here and my heart fills with hatred for all that he represents. He tries to drag the woman away from the grave. She wriggles free and stumbles forward for a last glance into the abyss. If I was like Grace, a monster in need of blood, I might let her live. Him on the other hand...

Though far away, he seems to notice my focused attention on him. He looks at me and I hold his gaze. There is no love in his hard face, only fear of the unknown. He pushes out his chest further. Chin up. Dominant, if only in his own, forced world. I don't challenge his strange behavior. I don't need to. He's uncomfortable locking eyes with me for this long and tears his eyes away from me to refocus on his wife, yanking her arm to leave. Her sunglasses fall to the ground. A badly make-up-covered shiner on her face says it all. Emma wasn't the only one suffering under his

225

'strong family leadership'. What a small-minded, weak man.

I watch them all leave. A giant tractor, its front filled with freezing dirt is Emma's only company taking away any romantic illusions from this graveyard. My lovely friend is gone.

A while passes and I finally force myself up and go to her grave. It's pretty. Under a big tree I can lean against. It steadies me. I stare at the freshly covered earth. Small snowflakes start dancing through the air. Serene and sad. I look from the fresh heap of dirt across the many tombstones. Some candles, some flowers, some lanterns. So many untold stories and so little time. Darkness settles around me. The day has given way to the night. My breath the only sign of life. I haven't moved in minutes, hours, centuries, I don't know anymore. But all of a sudden the wind carries news of a last adventure.

There, at the entrance, the tall, broad-shouldered monster waits. Far away. But clearly connecting only with me. A challenge. An invitation to follow? I give Emma's resting place one last glance before I push myself off the tree.

"I guess I'll see you very soon, old friend." I tell Emma and follow the ancient killer to whatever brutal fate he has in store for me.

CHAPTER 43: LAST STAND - NESS

Atlanta's blinking lights sparkle with dimmed muteness far on the horizon as if they too stopped caring. I follow the monster out of the comfort of the small cemetery, around several street corners. With each turn, more urban neglect comes out to greet me.

He disappears into the darkness of an old train terminal and I hesitate. An image flashes through my mind's eye. A pair of ice-blue eyes on a subway car across, heading in the opposite direction. I swallow with sadness. Grace is gone. He likely killed her and I will never know. Maybe I can return the favor.

This train depot was built on top of an already existing, albeit outdated one, that was left behind to the mercy of the elements. So, it created a pocket of a forgotten world below. The darkness is all-consuming as I step into it and my eyes are so slow to adjust. So very human. What am I doing? I am following Death yet again.

I glance behind me to take in the city. The snow drops heavier now, with some resolute resolve. This is very rare for Atlanta. I can only remember snow from one occasion other and it melted the next morning. This seems to be the city's way of weeping with me for the perfect life I've lost. I pull myself out of the state of self-pity and step forward into the cavernous abyss. Tall ceilings span across a great expanse, covered in bat-shit and graffiti. I don't see the puddle in front of me, but I hear my foot connecting with the thin, crackling layer of ice that covers it. It shatters. I move ahead on the frozen, precarious ground.

I can't see the monster anymore, but I know he wants me to follow. All I have to do is wait. So I stand, watching my breath clouds dissipate into the gloom, and glance around the towering pillars. They're making him even harder to spot, but then I catch a glimpse of his long, ragged-worn coat moving behind the farthest one on the right. I press on.

I don't know what I will do once I catch up with him. Shaking his hand seems out of the question. A simple hello does as well. Do I ask what happened to Grace? Do I get to? Will he just finish the job and kill me as well? I guess it doesn't matter. Something drives me forward like an invisible force and I don't fight it.

We walk and walk for hours. We leave behind the skyline and the train yards, down through the broken system of cultural integration, and beyond my dreams, until I spot a building emerge in my line of sight. I've heard of this place. I thought it wasn't real. A true urban legend. Candler Mansion stands with stark pride against the moonless night. It looks like an abandoned castle after Sleeping Beauty had been long rescued by her prince, stolen away, and left her old prison to the indifference of natural decay. The structure is intricate and must have been breathtaking during its heyday. It still is, but in a very different way.

I watch the creature sneak through the boarded-up entrance inside. I approach with caution. I know that he'll kill me slowly. He'll probably enjoy it too. But I cannot help myself. I want to follow. I need to know.

The structure next to the main building is smaller and seems like a much better alternative than blindly following the monster on his nefarious terms. It's a beautiful, partially nature-reclaimed, decrepit greenhouse. Parts of the roof have been damaged and fallen, making it look a bit like a cracked tooth. I enter, utterly aware of every step I take. I see debris littered across the floor, though dusted with snow. I'm sure there are legions of rusted nails ready to jump at the opportunity to impale my feet.

As I enter fully, I take in the melancholic glory of this place. Snow gently falls through the remainder of the ceiling. Plants are everywhere. A bramble of weeds, wood, and thorns. A forlorn tangle of early 20th century abandonment.

I hear a loud step behind me and whip around. At least I want to be ready. My breath halts. I peer into the darkness. But I can't find the set of cruel, silver eyes. Another noise makes my head spin in the opposite direction and my heart flutters. Pure adrenaline.

A shuddering breath of relief and shock shoots through me and a whimper of gratitude escapes my lips. I can't believe my eyes. Grace steps towards me from the rubble. She's limping and hurt, but she's alive. I feel my heart again. The elation is almost unbearable and I let tears of relief fall freely as I lock her into a tight embrace. My fingers interlace in her hair and I kiss her cheek, her head, and finally her lips. She smiles at me, albeit weakly.

"I thought you were dead." I croak out and I don't sound like myself anymore. This beautiful woman has cracked something wide open within me. Without her, I was ready to die myself and follow a sinister monster without a second thought. With her by my side, my heart is full. I finally understand the small imperfections love has to offer and how they add to a kaleidoscope of joy.

I pull back and take her in. Her awkward stance, her injured shoulder, her wounded torso. She's still bleeding. Concern ripples through me as I realize just how hurt she is. My eyes widen with the obvious question.

"Why are you not healing?" I ask and can't tear my eyes from hers. Her small smile is lopsided and sad.

"I figured out how to die." She rasps and my heart skips a beat. No. Not an option. I won't permit it.

I shake my head in disbelief. Brow to brow, in need of connecting with her cool skin. I don't want to let her go. I want more time with her. I need more time with her.

"You can't die on me." I order, sounding foolish but meaning every word.

I kiss her with all of my stubborn hopes and dreams of eternal life together. She lets me and gently opens my lips with hers. Her tongue connects with mine and gently teases it in play. The kiss is short but deep and full of longing and love. I squeeze her a bit tighter towards me when I suddenly hiss in a small pain. Something stings

229

me. My fingers rise to my lips. Blood pulses through the small hurt and I look at her.

"You bit me." I say, stating the obvious.

She holds out her hand in invitation as she bites her own lip bloody.

"I had to. Do you trust me?" An odd question at an odd moment. But I do. I would do anything for her. I nod and she pulls me in again, kissing me and passionately mingling both of our blood on our lips. Just a little, but I see her beautiful eyes spark and I adore her in wonder. More passion knits us together in a tangle of roving arms and kisses in the middle of this forgotten place. The cold seems to have disappeared. All I feel is her.

She pulls back a little and takes my hands into hers as she wipes the last bit of blood from my lips.

"We have to kill it." There is seriousness in the words. But lightness covers it up. I think she's trying to hide something from me. But I can't quite figure out what it is. I nod in agreement, knowing that no matter what, the ancient creature will murder callously until we stop it. So we have to put an end to its existence.

"I know." I tell her, my brows bunching together in determination and worry. My eyes are locked on hers, taking in every minuscule detail. Something deep down tells me this might be my last chance to do so.

"You figured out how, haven't you?" I ask her and the cold realization hits me. She knows how to die and she knows how to kill the creature. What is she not telling me? What part of the puzzle am I too blind to see?

Something makes Grace stiffen. She can feel him. He's close. He's here.

"Yes." She breathes and her pupils dilate slightly.

A THUD reverberates above us and our eyes dart towards the noise. Hovering on the glass, slowly CRACKING it, is the monster, both blades in his hands, ready to sing.

Grace shoves me forward as she draws a large blade from her back. I've never seen that wicked sword.

230

"Run!" She tells me and I obey, hurriedly stumbling into a sprint. Grace follows, close on my heels. It's difficult to navigate through the tangled root systems of dead plants, frozen statues, shattered glass, and old furniture, but I hurdle over any obstacles as fast as I can manage.

Above us, I can catch sight of the dark shadow jumping with supernatural agility and strength. He easily outpaces us. This is a game to him. He'll pin us wherever he wants to and then force one of us to watch as he kills the other. "Faster!" I'm so glad Grace interrupts my train of thought as I try to push my human body to its brink. Against two immortals, it's not very impressive.

I hear something zoom near us and duck on instinct. The shattering explosion of glass comes from behind. Not far at all. Shards rain down on Grace as the monster lands close to us.

I glance at her and see a trail of blood running down her perfect face like a tear. This ancient thing can hurt her, I realize. She figured it out. The thoughts dance around in my head. I couldn't kill her no matter what I did. Nothing could. But a tiny fragment of glass, aimed by him, another immortal, injures her without trouble. Fear runs through me and spreads. Nothing stopping it from reverberating through every cell of my body.

My eyes search the greenhouse tunnel behind us, the small pathway between the glass domes, but I can't locate the creature. Anywhere. Where did that ancient asshole go? Grace bumps into me, trying to shove me along a bit, but something doesn't seem right. She holds her impressive sword in one hand a small curved blade in the other. She looks like a dark mistress of death. Stunning. I might be a human, but even I won't go down without a fight. I look around us and pick up an old wooden stool leg from the pile of detritus on the floor. It has two lovely, rusted nails sticking from it. It's no sword, but it'll have to do.

"I really want a life with you." I tell her, determined to fight for that wish.

"Now that I'm dying, I finally understand it all." She says and I don't know where to start. Can I tell her she'll be fine? I need her to be.

"I want a life with you too." She concludes and our eyes find each other's in the darkness. Another loud crash of glass and the dark figure lands in front of us, slowly rising to his full, impressive height, blocking any way forward. Grace lunges. Slices. She ignores her pain and dashes sideways. She's marvelous. Her movements are so smooth and meticulous.

A yelp escapes him. One of her blades must have landed and cut flesh. I spot it. His arm is bleeding. She can hurt him too. It's a comfort. If she can hurt him, she can kill him. I'll distract him. I'll be the bait if I need to be and follow Grace off a cliff.

"Run!" She yells at me and her beautiful face twists in a pained expression.

I back up and hurl myself into the next tunnel. An entire system of fragile glass walkways, connecting like spider webs from glass dome to glass dome. Mostly broken.

The dark figure parries with nimble wrists. He spins one shiny knife, catching the light as a distraction as he throws the second. I only catch a glimpse of it, running forward.

But I hear Grace scream in pain. The second knife must have found its mark.

"You're not strong enough to kill me." He tells her way too matter-of-factly. He's right. I know it deep down. I turn and watch as Grace clenches her stomach, blood soaking her shirt.

"I don't need to be." She jumps and slices at the same time. Up. More glass breaks in a shower of silver, covering the monster and drawing small spots of blood from his skin.

He lowers his head. Covering himself with his arms.

Grace uses the moment and runs to follow behind me.

I continue to retreat back into the adjacent room. A stunning place. It reminds me of a large, church-like chapel. The glass-domed ceiling is also already partially broken. A set of stairs leads up to it as though it was showing us the way to heaven. Where is this going? But I don't think I'll get an answer. This place has witnessed many stories over the years but has clearly been forgotten for some time. I'm not sure who would even know where these stairs lead. Grace glances at me and I understand. I start ascending carefully, first making sure that the wood isn't too rotten to hold me.

"Go!" She screams and I climb faster, my little makeshift stool leg weapon dropped at the bottom like a discarded toy. I'm still not entirely sure what her plan is, but I can trust her. I can do that.

Another jump up, past a missing step and I hold onto the beams that support the dome high above. Rusty metal scrapes my palms. I swing my feet, the distance below significant enough to make my stomach drop. I focus and swing again, drawing my knees up to gain momentum. I manage to catch hold of a broken window and pull myself through.

The night is quiet up here. I lie as flat as I can on the beams looking down. Eerie. I can feel it. A pulse in the air. Not quite audible, but very present nonetheless. I scan the grounds.

There. Grace hauls herself inside the glass chapel, holding her middle with her injured arm.

The dark figure follows on her heels, ready to claim two lives, but still taking his time. Blow after blow, he outmatches her and she lets him, slowly guiding him to a spot right below me. What is her plan?

"Do you trust me?" I hear her shout and I know she's talking to me. Why does she repeat the question? Of course, I do. She knows that. Why remind me? Another few steps and I know she's luring the creature to this spot on purpose. He follows so willingly, and I really hope Grace knows what she is doing or else we're both really, really dead, very, very shortly.

Another slice from the dark figure's knife hits home and Grace's shoulder bleeds. She dives and rolls to avoid her

233

opponent. As she does, her finger scalpel slices his ankles with precise attention. He's brought down to the ground and kneels immediately. A SCREECH escaping his distorted face. Hope flares up within me. She can do it. She can kill this beast.

"Vanessa?!" She shouts again and I hear the strain in her voice. I rise to attention. I scoot forward peering down through the broken glass. A large hole spreads through the ceiling in front of me. Right where she's leading the ancient vampire. Our eyes meet and slowly her plan clicks in for me. No. I can't do that. Before I have any more time to contemplate, the dark figure follows Grace's eyes and jumps up. One move and he has reached the stairs. He'll be right upon me, killing me first.

Grace knows it too and I see desperation rising in her face as she picks up the stool leg I abducted earlier. My preternatural love is attempting to fight a superior immortal with nothing but a few rusted nails stuck through a piece of rotten wood. Now I know we've lost. I watch her rally her strength trying to defend me from the impending, final leap the monster is certainly about to take.

"Jump!" She shouts at me and I am only half shocked. I realized she wanted me to partake in her little plan, but letting myself fall? From this height? I am human. What would that even accomplish?

I can do this one thing, I think. I can trust her. He'll kill us both anyway. So I inhale deeply and scoot further. Right above them.

Grace lunges forward. All her strength in a few last movements. She lands in front of the dark figure between him and me, blunt wooden stake in hand. How poetic and utterly cliché. A stake. I huff a laugh.

So does the monster. But the sound of his is much more abhorrent. He slowly corners her up the stairs. Each step one move closer to ending us both.

"I'll catch you. I promise." She huffs into the cold air, doubt and fear lacing each word. I rise to my feet. If I die today, I will do it with intention and try my best. I will trust her. Grace retreats another step and the monster follows. One small glance up at me tells me all I need to know. Love. She loves me as I love her. Grace has a small tear in the corner of her eye as she smiles at me.

"Now." She almost whispers but I can read the word off of her lips. Love makes you do crazy things. One last exhale and I let myself fall.

CHAPTER 44: TURN

Everything is in slow motion. I feel the fall. Some small pieces of glass break off the rim with me and join in formation for the long dive down. It's surreal. A few days ago, I talked people off the ledge for a living. I adhered to the rules. I wrote them. Now I'm the one jumping. I love the fall. The feeling of complete loss of control and gaining the ultimate freedom at the same time.

I watch Grace twist, unable to do anything about it as her lethal plan unfolds. Her back is toward the dark figure, who embraces her in a sharp, deadly hold, one of his knives to her throat. I'm still sailing through the air excruciatingly slowly when I finally see what she has been working towards. Grace's hands place the wooden stake onto her own chest. My landing is the final blow driving it through her own heart, just as she opens her arms to catch me and hold me tightly one last time. My eyes go wide with horror knowing the inevitable end and I land, my weight and momentum piercing the stake through her. Deep and true.

I hear her inhale in my ear, feeling her breath and her lips on my skin. I scream.

All three of us tumble and roll in a comical clutch of death. In one last act of love, Grace's fingers grab a hold of mine and force the stake deeper through herself, all the way through the ancient monster clasping us both from behind her.

As we come to a stop, something changes within me. A sensation, a smell, I cannot tell what it is. But I feel an urge of some feral kind. Grace's hands release their hold on me and as I manage to scramble to my knees, I spot her. Throat slit from the creature still pinned to her body. Blood flowing freely down her neck taking its time, finding each crevice and seeping into the fabric of her clothes.

Her eyes fix solid silver onto me and every so slowly change back to their stunning blue color. Beautiful in death. I watch them dull as my last hopes of happiness fade with her.

I SCREAM with an agony I've never known. Broken. Not empty anymore. I am filled with a newborn rage, all-consuming and raw.

"No. You have to come back to me. You always come back to me." I sound different. My voice is stronger. I cup Grace's face in my hands. Stroke her cheeks and memorize the feel of her velvet soft skin. Tears should be running down my face but I don't feel any. I only feel heat rising within the hollows of my stomach. Burning.

I hear labored breathing below Grace from the monster, still pinned between the rubble and the stool leg I helped drive through him.

"She won't this time." His voice wheezes, close to death himself and waning with every passing second.

"She figured it out. So smart of her. To have us both die for you. You'll be very strong." His words ring in my ears. They're still very clear and for the past hour I've been putting things together piece by piece. But he continues, sparing me any additional confusion.

"You gain the strength of the one you kill." Miraculously my rage grows to unknown heights.

"You killed her. Only another immortal can kill..." My spitting words flutter out when the true, cold realization hits me. I sob, but where tears should be, my skin feels like perfect marble. The creature coughs a dark, blood-spattered laugh.

"Oh no, darling. You did. Both of us died at your hands while our blood flowed in your veins."

A bitter frenzy fills my head with a pounding so loud that I don't know where to move to make it stop. He's right. They both bit me. I tasted his blood in the waters of the aquarium. And Grace... She knew. She damn well knew. This was her plan. Dying. She's wanted to die all along. It the end, she still picked death over me. She could have...the Thought breaks off again and I remember our last kiss. Her small bite stinging my lips gently, but enough to break my skin, taste my blood, and give me hers. She knew and chose to leave me alone in this world. Like her father did to her.

My scream ECHOES through the remaining glass, as my hands shoot out and clasp around the monster's throat. I've never felt anything like this before. True power. I can feel the flesh melt between the smallest movement of my squeezing fingers. I don't take my time to enjoy killing him, but I do pull and rip out his throat from the bone, leaving nothing behind.

His head falls slack to one side and I feel a small amount of gratification. Icy silence shrouds us as snowflakes slowly dance around me. My breath is my only company as I stare at the two dead creatures.

The night is young. My body knows this on instinct. A prickling sensation of endless possibilities. I walk home through the snow. Each step leaves a small footprint, keeping my new, deadly secret. Grace knew. She knew if she did this to me, I would be alone. Would have to be alone like she was. Yet, I love her, and miss her. She's all I can think about until this new, burning pain revisits my body. It drives me mad. I try to take in air and ignore it, but it comes again and again. Stronger each time.

When I reach the house, I debate not entering, but the curtains of the kitchen window flutter softly in the cold wind. Just hours ago, I climbed down that side of the house.

I enter the kitchen. A newfound numbness hits me like a punch in the gut as I see my mother in a pool of her own blood. For a second, I am frozen to the spot. Unable to move. I just breathe, no tears coming to my new, sharply focused eyes. My mother must have picked up Emma's letter from the trash. It's on the kitchen table and I pick it up and I slowly walk over to my mom's body. I fold it and pocket it. No need to read it, I know the words.

"Last night upon the stair,
I saw a girl who wasn't there.

239

I squint my eyes shut, willing this to be a dream. A nightmare I can wake up from at any moment. Not real. Not real at all. A flash of Grace's stunning silver eyes visits my mind but is gone equally fast.
"She wasn't there again today,
Oh, how I wish she'd go away."
Another moment flares through my brain. A stolen kiss on a roof. Soft and still hesitant with shyness.
"She loves a songbird, pure and fair.
A nightingale, a song of air.
Of Innocence, of life and yearning."

The burning sensation makes me hallucinate. I can barely see straight. Is this hunger?
"A bird of love, but dead come morning."

I bend down and touch my mother's blood with shaking fingers. I can't. I love my mother, I think, but the burning is unyielding. Merciless and ancient. I have no choice but dip my fingers carefully. I feel the dried, crusty fluid, repulsed and shocked. But the burning is stronger. I inhale deeply and have no control left as I lick my fingers clean.

The night went on. It's almost dawn now and I am not sure I can stand this strange new existence. But before I decide what I can do about it, I have this new urge within me that must be addressed. And there is one specific place I have in mind, that may just deserve this specific kind of attention.
A RING.
The doorbell CHIRPS again as I press it down a second time. A tired, drained, and confused middle-aged man opens the door. Blinking through his receding slumber, adjusting nothing about his disheveled existence but his mustache. Emma's father.
The recognition hits him. He knows he's seen me somewhere before. I don't care much about whether he can actually place me at his daughter's funeral. I care

240

about his cruel treatment of her. His loveless, callus way of driving her to suicide one day at a time. For the first time in my likely long, immortal life, I make my pupils turn. His eyes widen as he stares into dead, cold silver. I am ready and I pounce.

EPILOGUE: A NEW LIFE - LUKE

The music is lively. It's almost impossible not to move at least your shoulders or tap a foot along. It was a great idea to have my friend's jazz quartet play at our engagement party. I'm not usually into these sort of things. A wedding, a rehearsal dinner, a bachelor party and an engagement party. That's so many parties. Usually, there's stress associated with one or several of them. I've been a groomsman before and once, for my brother, a best man. Something always goes wrong and causes drama.

But not today. This barn-style warehouse in the middle of the city is gorgeous. It smells of cedar and the red velvet cookies that keep being passed around. Instead of champagne giving me a headache, I stick to beer and love it. It's so refreshing in the humid summer heat. Even at night, it's hot outside and an army of talkative cicadas share their story without invitation. Somehow they fit in time the music. It makes me smile. I'm wearing a suit today, but not the stuffy kind. I found myself a light blue linen set with a white shirt and the most comfortable shoes. I never thought I would like this, but it's breezy and perfect. It was my bride's idea. To not stuff me into something that looks like a costume and makes me feel stiff. I think of her and smirk. Then I see her standing in the crowd, laughing with my parents. Her hair is swept up for the occasion, but a stubborn curl still bounces along with her exuberant happiness. Ally is a light.

I never thought I could love again after Ness. First, she broke my heart, then her own, and when I saw her again after, she was something else entirely. Otherworldly and entirely alone. Of course, I still loved her. I will always love her. But it's different now. For the past six months, I was her only friend. I kept my boundaries clear. So did she. But we agreed on a few important things. We can help each other. She is the best thing I could ever hope to study to push my immortality research forward, and I am the only person she can be entirely honest with.

We realized quickly that we can't repeat Grace's mistakes and have to learn as much as possible about her...condition. She also can't be just a sitting duck. If Grace's uncle knew where to find her, others are out there. Somewhere. That's when we started looking for a trainer and met Ally. This gorgeous, radiating woman I soon get to call my wife is an Army vet who did two combat tours and now teaches self-defense classes for women. She built her own business and now runs a martial arts gym next door. When we first spotted her, she knew something was different about Ness, but never asked. She just taught her the basics. Slow and steady. Now the two of them train three times a week and have advanced to a wild array of fighting techniques. She knows Ness isn't human. But neither of us ever told her the specifics. For Ally, it didn't matter. She saw someone so deeply traumatized and hurt that she wanted to help build her strength back up through physical control. It's apparently also fun for her to have an opponent who can at any time entirely outmatch her and keep her on her toes.

Ally likes Ness and trusts me. She knows her heart belongs to a dead woman and that mine has been reborn with Ally. We even invited Ness to join the festivities, but it was a little too much for her. So as per usual, when there are too many people, she sits on the roof, feet dangling off the side, sulking into the starry night. I can see her through the skylight. She's not hiding.

Ally follows my gaze and jerks her head for me to go check on her. I smirk. Her kindness baffles me.

The sky is beautiful tonight. The stars glimmer above and are clearly visible even in the middle of the city.

"The blue looks good on you." Ness muses, her voice a little sad. I get it. This could easily have been our engagement party. I sit next to her and hand her a small cocktail glass. Her eyebrows rise sky-high.

"You're a scientist. The human food aversion should be in the vampire 101 category." I smile at her and push the little cup closer, pulling out a flask for myself.

She sniffs carefully, ready for the usual gag reflex to alert her of just how vile any mortal cuisine is. Her eyes widen. "Blood?" I wink.

"My uncle has a farm. He brought the burgers so I asked him for a small favor." I raise my flask, my favorite, aged scotch in it and we clink.

"To a long and happy marriage." She says and I know she means it, underlying sadness notwithstanding.

"Thank you." I tell her and squeeze her shoulders.

"You don't have to be here, you know? I get it." I continue but she shrugs it off.

"Of course, I'll be here. I want you both to be happy. You know that. It's just...not today." She stops herself and I gently nudge her.

"It's selfish." She chastises herself and I spot the tiniest glimpse of her razor-sharp canines.

"Now that you two are getting married, I'll be all alone. It's been over six months and we haven't found any others."

Ah. Of course. I understand that one. We've been searching the Internet, even the deepest corners of the dark web. Between the two of us, we've read every book and created an extensive database of clues that could compete with my thesis.

"Despite your best efforts, I'm still in your life and I still love you." I smirk at her and she smiles back lopsidedly.

"We will find them. I promise. We will find more stubborn, strange immortals that will ignore every piece of good advice." She huffs at me. Teasing her like this has become my favorite pastime. I hope my promise won't be empty and that I can deliver on it. We've been exploring what feels like every available source for any signs of someone like her. Nothing. I understand how she is losing hope. I put my arm around her shoulder again and look into her silver eyes.

"Don't fret, little monster. You're not alone."

ACKNOWLEDGEMENTS

I never wanted to write a book. As a screenwriter and director, this isn't my format. But one of my friends encouraged me to write this specific story into a novel and I'm grateful that he did. I learned so much about this world and each of the characters. I hope you, dear reader enjoyed it.

Inspired by my lovely, late friend, Daniel, whose humor was too infectious for this world and who fought so valiantly with depression, 'Death of a Nightingale' is an escapist take on a very sad reality. We still don't talk about suicide enough. The shame around mental health and depressive thoughts can be debilitating and numbing. That's why I wanted to wrap these thoughts into a shell of escapism and absurdity and wrote a vampire story about it. Pieces of my dear friend are all over it and so is his smile.

I would like to thank very much my lovely editor, Chris Tetzlaff who started speed-editing on strange deadlines and wild requirements. Thank you! Another big, 'so many thank yous' goes to my Swiss Army Knife manager Jon Hersh for his unshakable patience over the last few years, his trust, and simply for believing in me and my art. All of us crazy story-tellers need someone to encourage us, push us forward, and sometimes guide us off a ledge. Also, thank you for indulging every insane idea that frequently crosses my mind and thinking about it before evaluating it properly.

I want to thank my patient and ever-loving family. My mother, a storyteller herself, brainstorms like the best of them. My grandfather still always lifts me up with love and patience, incredible German cooking, and a sly hand at card games. My cousins, who are really my siblings, thank you for embracing and loving a fantastical odd-one-out. My closest friends, sorry for never shutting up about stories. Unfortunately, I don't think I ever will:).

Death of a Nightingale is a trilogy. To give you a little taste of it, here is how the poem continues through part two and three.

Part One:
Death of a Nightingale:

Last night upon the stair,
I saw a girl who wasn't there.
She wasn't there again today
Oh, how I wish, she'd go away.
She loves a songbird, pure and fair
A nightingale, a song of air,
of innocence, of life and yearning,
a bird of love, but dead, come morning.

Part Two:
Hawk of the Night:

Now hawk, a hunter,
Prey in sight.
A bird of wonder,
Bird in flight.

Stronger now, the other side.
With a lovely, human heart of might. Of romance, full of hope and light,
To set ablaze the darkest night.

Part Three:
Crow of Darkness:

Last night upon the stair
I saw a crow just waiting there. When I came back next night at three
The crow was waiting there for me. Peculiar bird of death, the crow to pick and lead my soul below, into the blackest night of hollow Where she alone can freely follow.

This is loosely based the first four lines on the "Antigonish", a poem from 1899 by the American educator and poet, William Hughes Mearns. It is also known as "The Little Man Who Wasn't There". It is in the public domain. The other parts of the poem were created for each of the books/films to summarize the journey of the main character.

If you or anyone close to you needs help

+988 is the international suicide prevention hotline.

If you want more information please visit:

www.suicidepreventionlifeline.org

Finito di stampare
nel mese di ottobre 2024
presso Rotomail Italia S.p.A. – Vignate (MI)